Skyline

Acclaim for

A Time of Angels

'Tender, witty and engaging'
J.M. Coetzee

'Announces the arrival of an exciting new talent'
Daily Mail

'A marvellous novel, written with style, gusto and immense charm'
Joanne Harris author of Chocolat

'A seductive fable offering an unusual well-written narrative'
Booklist

'A bewitching tale ... It's nothing short of heavenly'
People Magazine

The Apothecary's Daughter

'A richly romantic tale of sexual awakening, love and betrayal'
J.M. Coetzee

'A wondrous narrative, a poignant complex drama, stitched
through with rich imagery and tenderness'
Sunday Independent

'Beautifully written ... the prose leaving a resonance in the mind
somewhat in the same way that, say, Turkish Delight leaves a
scented richness on the tongue'
Irish Examiner

'A languid and highly spiced drama'
Sunday Times

A Quilt of Dreams

Also by Patricia Schonstein

A TIME OF ANGELS
THE APOTHECARY'S DAUGHTER
A QUILT OF DREAMS

www.patriciaschonstein.com

Skyline

PATRICIA SCHONSTEIN-PINNOCK

african sun press

© 2000 Patricia Schonstein-Pinnock
ISBN 978-1-874915-13-3

Published in 2007 by African Sun Press
P O Box 16415
Vlaeberg 8018
Cape Town South Africa
www.afsun.co.za

Publishing history:
First published in 2000 by David Philip Publishers
Second impression 2002
Third impression 2004
Fourth impression 2005

Swedish translation: Tranan 2002 and En bok för alla 2006
French translation: L'éclose editions 2004
Italian translation: Il cielo di Cape Town. Editrice Pisani 2005

Layout and design by Scarlet Media. www.scarletmedia.co.za
Cover photographs © Gaelen Pinnock

Thousands of children were forced to take part in Mozambique's sixteen-year civil war (1976-1992) which brought social and economic ruin to the region.

Most were abducted from their homes and made to play a cruel and brutal role in the war.

This book is dedicated to them, and to all child victims of war.

Chapter 1

This is how our father leaves home. He does it simply and without any explanation. He just does not come home one Friday night. I realize he's gone for good because there is an emptiness in the air which was not there before. Now there will be no more fighting and the arguments which tear through the flat will become still.

This is how we are positioned: I am sitting on the couch, aware of the traffic outside, as I always am. My sister, Mossie, is on the floor playing poker with two imagined friends. Our mother is huddled up over the phone. There is no wind. The moon is not visible in the night sky.

She has been on the phone since ten o'clock, when it became clear to her that he was not coming back. She has phoned the Kimberley Hotel, the Stag's Head Bar and Club Georgia. Her hope is that he is pissed and leaning up on a bar somewhere. Now she is phoning hospitals and police stations in case he has had an accident.

I wonder why she is bothering. They are not good friends and all that comes between them is broken and ugly. There is no tenderness.

I trace the patterns on the arm of the couch with my finger: Bird. Branch. Grapes. Entwined leaves. The cloth is worn thin and I pull at a thread. Finally I get irritated and spell it all out for her: Can't you see he's gone? He wasn't in an accident. He hasn't been hijacked. He just hasn't come home. He's left you. Us. He's gone.

I do not say this in a pleasant way. I say it to hurt her because she has driven him away. But she's not listening and carries on with her strange hunt for him.

She lights up a cigarette even though there's one already lit and smoking in the saucer. Her hair is all over the place. She's such a wreck I can't stand looking at her. Outside the traffic is screaming. It doesn't always scream. Sometimes it howls. Sometimes it runs smoothly. Sometimes it sounds like a woman singing. Tonight it's screaming and filling the flat with rush and panic.

She draws on her cigarette, holds the smoke inside. The traffic is crying now and its sorrow pours onto the veranda and in through the windows, splashing everything with tears. The traffic is the wail of a madonna stripped and bleeding.

I go through to lie on my bed and leave the light off. I watch the city lights move across the ceiling, splintering up the darkness. It's not ever really dark in our room. Even with the lights off, the cars and neons and street lights leave a glow all the time. The city pours in, swirls around, stains everything with paint thrown against a wall, running down, mixing.

Mossie creeps onto my bed. Her face is wet. Why're

you crying, Mossie? There's nothing to cry about. I wipe her cheeks. She holds me and in the half light makes her sound for Daddy. I sit up and push her hard so she falls off the bed. Don't ever say that name! You hear me? He's gone! Gone! I shout at her. I grab her and shake her by the shoulders, then push her from me again so she stumbles backwards and hits against the wall. You never say that word Daddy again! You hear me? That's a dead word!

Then, even in the half-dark, in the glow of the traffic and street lights, I see she is confused and sad. So I hold her and rock her and hum a bit. The traffic is a flock of birds crying in the evening, going home. Don't cry, Mossie. Don't cry.

She doesn't understand. You know how she is. But I make her understand. Daddy is gone and we never say his name again.

The first painting, titled *It is the Cape Town City*, resembles Umberto Boccioni's *Street Noises Invade the House*.

Brisk and sometimes explosive brush strokes capture the dynamism of a rushing city, full of movement, terror and expectation.

A girl looks down from the veranda of a block of flats into the street below. Surrounding buildings lean towards her, making her the focus of the picture.

Colours carry an orchestration of African city-sound to the centre of the painting. Azures, plumbago-blues and fire-yellows weave through traffic choruses with the beating of goat hide drums and rhythms of kwaito. A cacophony of cars and rushing people swirls around in a tempest of colour: granadilla-orange, placenta-red, leguaan-blue and the browns of Kalahari sand.

We might imagine we hear, caught within the mixing of golden-yellow and purple, the soft tinkling of someone's brass bracelets.

Chapter 2

I meet Raphael at the gate after school. We walk down Orange Street and sit on the steps of the Christian Science church, waiting for Mossie.

He has an orderly life with a mother who bakes good cakes and plays bridge three times a week. His father left home in an orderly way. He died by drowning and left insurances and bank balances with a beautiful house for his wife and son to live in. Silverware and Persian rugs and carved furnishings make up the stage set Raphael lives in. With a dream sometimes of a man drifting slowly down into deep water; silver bubbles singing silently out of his mouth; his eyes startled; his hair flowing upwards; polished black shoes weighing him down; his arms reaching up as if in praise; a dark tie waving from his neck like an underwater fern. All this in a deep, blue lake.

Our mother never speaks to Raphael. She greets him when he comes in and out or if she sees him in town somewhere. That's all. I don't know who she talks to, really, because she hasn't got any friends. Sometimes I wish she also didn't come home ever again. Then it would just be me and Mossie and we'd do fine together. I'd care for her as I already do and everything would be much better, calmer, more orderly.

The New Horizons bus pulls up and we wait for Mossie to get off. Your bag, Mossie! I shout, but the bus is pulling off and once again it's too late.

Why do you always leave your bag, you rubbish? I shout at her and she laughs. You know how Mossie laughs. She throws her head from side to side and the sun catches her golden curls. I hold her hand and we all cross the road.

Do you want to take your stuff to school in a checkers packet, hey Mossie? Do you want to look like a bergie with all your stuff in a dirty old plastic bag?

She waves her arms around. She wants me to know plastic bags are better than school bags. And if you leave them on the bus no one sweats about it. I give her a shove.

The Nigerian crosses the other way. He smiles at us, smiles all around us with big, white teeth, but says nothing. His long, bright robe and cotton hat glow against his black skin.

We buy Cokes at 7Eleven and sit outside drinking, watching the flow of cars move through Long Street and split up at the intersection. I'm used to the traffic and the way it washes through my mind, swirling with changing rhythms. It is a moving, liquid, smooth and soothing music; a song of haunting sounds and hootings woven from the speed and rushings of the city. The traffic is a song which plays my feelings as though they were a string instrument or distant drum. It erases all silences within me.

It's nearly six and Raphael has to go home. He kisses me, right here outside 7Eleven, with everyone watching. He kisses my face then bows to kiss my hand. I give him a push and we laugh.

Mossie and I go up to our flat. This is Skyline at the top of Long Street. We live on the fifth floor and can see the sea from our veranda. Sun comes through our windows all morning. It plays on the walls, paints with long tendrils of light against shadow.

This joyous painting, *It is the Fine Young Man*, carries the same lightness and spontaneity as Marc Chagall's *The Fiddler*, upon which it is based.

Here, though, the fiddler is a young man wearing Levi jeans with a smudge of red as a shirt.

The full moon rises in the sky, an opulent yellow against a deep, metal-blue night.

In the foreground and background are low-roofed, Cape Dutch buildings painted with strong strokes of wetland-green and green-blues.

In mimicking the Chagall, the artist gives the impression that the young man is magically supported in the air.

Chapter 3

From outside, Skyline looks like a patchwork quilt draped from the sky. Different curtains and coverings hang at the windows, so you'll see a pinned-up blanket or Java print here and a curtain hanging off its rail there. Some curtains are short, some sag. There are white curtains, faded curtains and torn curtains. Some panes are covered in newspaper and broken windows are closed with cardboard. Soft lace billows out into the wind and a shirt hangs out to dry. There's a *For Sale* sign against one window and a board with big red letters advertising *Flats to Let* at another.

The verandas are stacked high with fridges, mattresses, bicycles, fold-up beds and armchairs which won't fit inside the crowded flats.

Most of the people who live here are illegal immigrants and refugees from the rest of Africa. The building is crowded with them sharing space, renting beds and corners of rooms. Not many have the right to be here and most of them carry forged papers or pay bribes to stay in the country. They arrive from all over Africa by taxi, by bus, by train. Some hitch rides on overland transporters. Many just walk. Their worlds cry through the stairwell like egrets flying home. Their worlds are like the traffic outside, weaving into plaited reeds and palm-frond rope. They flow over me with the glitterings of wind chimes trembling in the wind:

chips of bronze, chips of copper, slithers of flattened tin, tinkling.

There is dust in these people: red dust and brown dust and dust from shrivelled riverbeds. They carry dust from the scorched fields of war. Some are powdered with coal dust and asbestos dust or dust from the old copper mines. There are those covered with the ash of bones left to the wind after mass killings. Others are dulled by the dusts of the Slim people who have wasted away. All come here looking for a new life.

This is Mr Mandela's country, they say. *So everything must be good.*

Under their western clothes, some are tattooed and cut with ritual scars. Some have ear lobes stretched and heavy with rings. Their hair is plaited or braided like rivulets running over granite koppies. They play music on drums and little whistles or xylophones which speak of sands and golden dates or reed boats paddled across rivers pulling in fish.

Their music makes each flat become a village with bellowing oxen coming home at night. Their drumming speaks in the ochre and mud of clay pots and baskets woven tightly to hold beer and sour milk.

A tin guitar twangs forlornly about a crowded shack in a Lusaka township. A small drum, plaited round its edge with twine and carried across borders, down footpaths and along highways, pounds out songs of migrations and moving nomads, about orange sands and shifting sheets of dunes peppered with the bones of lost travellers.

There always seems to be someone new in the block. I might see someone just once and never again. A man in a white vest might lean on his veranda looking down into the traffic and up to the sky, all day long. He'd blend in or disappear so I need never know where he comes from, where he goes.

The guys who work at the Shell garage over the road call Skyline the Africa Junction: *You see! The whole of Africa is running into the country and to here at the top of Long Street. Do they think Cape Town is the big hotel with the free jobs? Or what they thinking? And do they think they can just come here from where they come from over Africa and take the people's jobs? What is going on with the government to let them in, hey?*

Now they selling passports and they buying your wives. Yes! They buy your wives, because they got a lot of money. So they buy your wife all the nice things. So your wife, she can't stay with you when you only got these small wages from the Shell garage. You see, they no good for us, these peoples. They must go back to their own country. They must go back to Congo or whatever.

Upstairs, in the flat above ours, we have a friend called Princess who plaits and beads hair at the Pan African Market. She has a small room there called the Afrika Salon where she cuts hair into Elvis, Sexy Boy and Harare Mamba styles. She is from Rwanda and is a big, strong person, always sweating; always brewing fragrant tea; always filled with lament.

You just call me Princess. I am Princess from Rwanda. You hear my name? Princess from Rwanda, and when you want to buy sleep, we can talk. What you asking? You asking of my children? No. I got no more daughters. My daughters they are all dead. No. We talk some other time about my daughters. We don't talk about this now.

Her arms move with her voice and her hands open and close like black lilies.

She rents out sleeping space to people who arrive in Cape Town with nowhere to go. They somehow find their way to her through a network which runs from the border to Skyline to refugee communities in Muizenberg and Melkbosstrand. They arrive without money but with stories written on the parchment of their hearts which they don't recite easily. They are stories which have crept out of the edges of civil wars and scattered into the fleeing wind. You can read the words in their eyes, stained by despair; in their mouths, silenced and tightened by horror. You can even read the words in their torn and weary clothes. Because they have no money, Princess binds them with unwritten contracts to come pay her when they have found work and somewhere to stay.

There are sweet-sellers living with her now who have settled in like her family. They are thin and tall and very black. She likes them close to her, breathes in deeply when they are beside her. They sell sweets and cigarettes on the Longmarket pavement and one of them sells black pens outside Home Affairs. When I see them I think of smooth-plumed cranes standing aloofly at the edges of a lake, glancing into the water for the movement of a fish.

In this, the third painting, *It is the Woman of Rwanda*, a fat, black woman sits on a wooden crate. Her legs are spread slightly apart, so her long and voluminous robe drapes down between her thighs.

She holds an open Chinese fan.

On her face are small, ritual scars, cut into her cheeks when she was a child. Her face is black-black. Her lips and the inside of her mouth are an evocative and erotic red.

The frenzied colours of her robe leap out from the canvas in their richness: mulberry-purple, burnt-ochre, paw-paw-orange and sacrificial-crimson.

We are reminded, though not by the woman's posture, nor by her race, of *Woman of Algiers* by Auguste Renoir. It is the facial expression, the look captured by the rich mouth, the profusion of colours which convey this similarity.

The frame of this picture is made from slightly rusted, flattened out Coca-Cola cans which detract somewhat from the timelessness of the woman's face.

Chapter 4

The sweet-sellers bring in a woman and her two children. They are thin and have bussed and hitched all the way down Africa from Sudan. They crossed borders without passports and without money, carrying just a bundle of thin blankets.

The woman shows us a letter from the imam of a mosque in Khartoum. It's just a small square of paper, folded over and over so that when you open it out it looks centuries old and grubby and very used. It's brown and stained by body oils and sweat and has the words *Sulamin, Cape Town* written in old-fashioned script.

We drink black tea and the sweet-sellers translate her story of Sudan and its war to us. Princess sways and mutters, clasps and unclasps her hands, wipes sweat from her face.

She leave the south when the rebels take her village. The rebels take her husband. So she leave with her children. She leave everything behind. All she take is her children and some bundles of things. The train is so full, even with soldiers, and there is nothing to eat, nothing to drink. All the people run to catch the train from the south to the north Sudan. This is the last train out because then the rebels blow the train line. They blow the train line at Ariat Bridge. Then after that people must walk to leave the south. And many they die because there is no water and the sun crack their skin and the feet swells up. In the north there is no place for these many peoples running from the south. They just live in the refugee camp with the scorpions. You know these camps for displaced peoples? They not so good. Now she move, this woman, like the wind, she move down away from our country. Like us too, moving from our country. You know the wind? It can carry nothing. Just some bit of paper with address or some name. This is the wind. Aaah.

The sweet-sellers talk all night about Sudan and Princess makes more black tea. She brews it with cinnamon and cardamom and cloves, then puts in lots of sugar so it tastes lovely. She sighs and heaves, clasps and unclasps her hands.

I look at the woman's shoes which she has placed neatly beside her sleeping mat. They have no colour left in them and are completely bashed up. They have taken on the weary shape of her leather feet. Her feet are hard and cracked. Her legs are dry and scratched with the markings of thorns and the merciless bushes which grow in dry places. Her children have no shoes. They have feet which look like worn-out little boots and their toes have no softness.

She curls up on a mat and her children lie beside her, making no sound. I have never seen children who make no sound, who just lean close to their mother and move with her movements. They don't laugh or cry and nothing shines from their eyes. They have come all the way down Africa, walking on their little boot-feet. They are lying here in front of me, not crying nor whimpering. They are not afraid but I know they should be afraid because they have seen their brothers cut down by rebels with machetes. They have seen their grandfather's arms hacked off and the stumps left bleeding.

Maybe they stopped being afraid the day their mother bundled them onto the last train across the Ariat Bridge; when she hurried them away from the war, hiding them here and there until the sound of gunfire was far. Maybe fear left them when they reached the refugee camp in Khartoum; or the day they left the camp, the day their mother said: *There is only sand for us here. We are leaving now. We are going to Nelson Mandela's country far away to the south, even farther than our home which is the most southern place we know. Nelson Mandela is the new King of Africa. He will call the rebels to return your father. They will free him clothed and well, not naked and bleeding. They will free him laughing and radiant, not blinded and stumbling. They will free him with his teeth still in his mouth and his limbs strong. He will not return broken. Oh no! And then I will cook some tender lamb or young goat and we will eat together at the fire. This is what the King, Mandela, will do for us.*

Tomorrow, she and her children will catch the train to Claremont to find the imam who will settle them in Cape Town. Someone will steal her bundle of blankets on the station platform. She will come back, one day, to pay for her night's sleep in Princess's flat and return the money the sweet-sellers lent her. Her children will show us their new shoes and smile.

Princess pours the last of the tea into my mug. I lean against the wall and think about war. These people say that war is a crocodile which is always hungry. It has dishonest eyes and a thrashing tail. It creeps up quietly while you wash at the river, while you pound your corn, while you rock your old mother in her time of dying.

It is with you always, war, waiting to explode your life and throw you down beside a riverbed to die. War wants death. War wants to quieten your mother's songs. War wants your sorrow.

We say goodnight.

The frame of the fourth picture is painted in bright enamels of erythrina-scarlet, lime-green and mango-yellow which contrast strongly with the more subdued colours of the painting itself.

A woman lies on the night sands of the desert under the full moon.

She is lying on her side with her head in the crook of her arm.

Her shawl and striped cotton dress cover her thin body like dry scrub covering a thirsty hill. In her dress we recognize the colours of semi-desert plants.

In the foreground is an empty food bowl of chipped enamel.

To the far right lies a machete.

Entering the painting from the side is a black-maned Barbary lion.

There is a similarity in this, *It is the Woman Travelling*, to Henri Rousseau's *Sleeping Gypsy*.

Chapter 5

Our mother comes home from work and says she's tired. She's tired in her body and tired in her mind and tired in her soul. She pours out a brandy and unwraps some take-away fish and chips.

I never help her. I don't know why I never help her. I just never do. Am I supposed to? Is there a partnership here? A sharing of nice things? Anyway, she never asks me for help or for company.

She drinks a few glasses of brandy while we eat everything, me and Mossie, because we're hungry. Then she washes the dishes and dries them and puts everything away. She tells us to put out the lights and go to bed and not to make noise because she wants to sleep. She takes her pills and closes herself in her room.

It's late and I'm lying on my bed listening to the traffic whirl and bluster. I hear her wake up and go to the bathroom. She's there a long time. I hear her come out. I hear her slippers against the passage floor. I hear her fall over. I lie still, poised like a leaf when the wind has no movement. I don't hear her again, so I get up to see what's happened.

She's knocked her head and is sprawled across the floor. I can't wake her up, so I shake her but that doesn't help. I lift her under the arms and drag her to her room. Why doesn't she wake up?

She groans and keeps mumbling: *You're so rough. So rough.* But I can't help it. She's hard to move. I've got her half on the bed and then I lift her legs up. Her nightie slips down and I see her body. I have never seen her without clothes on because she always covers herself in front of us. She has small, flat, white breasts. She is thin and her skin is pale and I am afraid to see her like this. She mumbles and calls my granny but she still won't wake up.

I pretend to be my granny: *Here I am.* That's what I say. *I'm here, now wake up! Wake up!* I shake her shoulders. I feel so stupid because if she wakes up she'll know I'm not my granny and she'll know I've seen her with her nightie half off. And anyway my granny lives in England, so there's no chance it would be her saying: *I'm here. I'm here. Now wake up.*

So I pull the blanket up and cover her. She's disgusting, that's what she is. And she stinks of brandy and cigarettes. The room is all aglow from the city lights. The room is darkness with light splashed against the walls, trickling down like tears. Why can't I have a normal life like everyone else?

In our room I know Mossie is awake. I know from the way she is breathing. She never gets up when this happens. She's too afraid. I don't say anything to make her feel better because I don't want to start explaining things to her. And anyway, our mother always wakes up next morning.

Except in the morning she never says anything. She acts as if nothing happened, as though it was a normal night with everyone having sweet dreams. But these are not dreams. They are not fogs creeping up from the wetlands to cover everything in freshness. These things that happen at night are real. And they're nothing to talk about. I'm ashamed of all this.

The fifth picture is drawn in charcoal on a sheet of cartridge paper which seems to have been crumpled and thrown down and then flattened out again.

Creases run through it, so the image of the weeping woman is somewhat broken.

She sits at a kitchen table with a bare bulb burning above her. On the table are a bottle of brandy, a glass, a packet of Camel cigarettes and a box of Lion matches.

The woman's hair has been brushed back into a plait and, although the medium and content of the picture are different, her face bears a striking similarity to that of Pablo Picasso's woman in *The Frugal Meal*. It is titled *She has Sorrow in the Kitchen*.

The charcoal, used sparingly here, with heavy hand there, covers a range of tones from burnt-acacia-grey to lead-grey.

Chapter 6

The first time I see Gracie is outside the Bead Shop. I'm leaning against the window, waiting for Mossie to choose beads, when I see a blind woman who's lost her way.

She taps a white cane against the ground while talking to her guide dog. I wonder what she wants in the Bead Shop. What could she do with all these colours? How will she see the sunlight shining through when she holds up an orange bead? What can green threaded next to umber threaded next to purple mean to her?

She taps with the cane. Her dog ignores me. Maybe I should help her. Maybe she'll fall over. You okay, lady? I ask and she says she's looking for the post office. She's way off track. It's up there in Loop Street. But I can't explain it without showing her, so I decide to walk up with her.

Wait here, I tell Mossie. Stay in the shop till I come back, you hear? Don't go out for anything. Understand? Don't let anyone call you out of the shop. I'll be back soon. Just wait here. And don't make trouble. Are you listening to me? She nods her head up and down and gives me a push. She wants me to know I don't have to tell her everything a hundred times, she's not thick.

I lead Gracie up to the post office in Loop Street. This is a new route for her and the guide dog, Molly. That's why they got lost.

Gracie and her husband have just moved into Skyline and she wants to sort out a phone. She takes a long time doing this and all the while I'm waiting I think of some better things I could be doing. When she's finished I take her back to Skyline and up to the first floor.

Her husband's leaning over the balcony looking down Long Street to the sea. Well, not really looking, because he's also blind. Anyway, he looks like he's staring down Long Street. He turns round to face me and shakes my hand.

I close my eyes and let him feel my face and hair with his soft, fat fingers. He holds my shoulder to know my height. His name is Cliff and his guide dog is called Beth.

Gracie and Cliff work for the police. She works on the switchboard and he's in public relations. Someone, one of their police friends I suppose, has already unpacked their things for them and straightened out the flat. Everything is really, really tidy and all in place. They have the entire Bible, a whole set of huge books, typed out in Braille. That must be so hard, reading with your fingers. Anyway, they show me round the flat. It's just like ours, but tidy, like I said.

There's a place for everything and everything is in its place, says Gracie. That is how they map out their flat, with tidiness. *If you pick up something, it must go back there when you finish.* They chart their whole world in threes and must always have three points to find their way. The robot – the letter box – the island in the middle of the road; the fridge – the stove – the sink; the tree outside the Palm Tree mosque – the electricity pole – another postbox; the door to Skyline – four steps up – the lift.

There's a basket for each dog. Their water bowls are full and their harnesses hang at the front door.

Cliff goes through to the kitchen and comes back with a tray of cups and a plate of cookies and wants to know if I want some tea and to taste the coconut macaroons he just made.

No, I don't mind having tea and biscuits, they look great. But I have to leave at six because Raphael is meeting me outside. You made these biscuits, Cliff? I ask him. They're nice. How do you know when they're cooked – I mean, you can't, um, you can't see them. Do you feel them with your fingers? Hot? How do you know when to take them out of the oven, so they don't burn?

He opens his mouth wide, laughing, and his eyes seem to look all over the place. Suddenly I like him a lot. And Gracie too. They are brave people.

Gracie and Cliff met in the police and fell in love when they felt each other's faces. But they could never do anything about it because she is coloured and he is white. Until 1990.

It's thanks to Mr Mandela that we could get married, says Cliff as he turns his face to where Gracie is sitting and she smiles towards his voice.

You know, scrapping apartheid. You want to know about the biscuits? They're so easy. Just the usual: flour, some coconut, sugar, mix it all up. Next time you come I'll show you.

You like baking? I shake my head but he can't see, so I tell him I don't.

No? Oh, it's great. I love it. I get my recipes off Woman's Hour *and a friend at work reads out the* My Family *cooking pages. It's relaxing. Helps me unwind. Mind you, it's no good for the tum. I mean, we are getting a bit portly, hey? Gracie? What d'you say, Gracie? We're growing out of everything, aren't we, love? So long as we feel good, I suppose it's okay, hey Gracie? Do I still feel good to you, Gracie?*

No, I never burn things. Gracie used to burn everything when we met. But I don't let her cook. I do all the cooking. She just eats. Don't you, Gracie, dear? You love it, hey? My cooking? Where are you Gracie? You listening?

Gracie is sitting on the couch, her feet up on the coffee table, grinning into the air. *Ja. I still love how you feel, Cliff.*

Okay, I must go now. See you again. I mean, well, yes, see you again.

Gracie and Cliff come to the door to say goodbye. He has his arm around her and she is smiling towards his face.

In this unframed painting, called simply *It is the Beauty,* a blind man stands in front of his blind wife who is sitting in a blue chair and who seems to look back at him, her head tilted slightly.

Behind them a window overlooks a garden described in wet, loose brush movements and offering escape from their dark worlds.

It is reminiscent of Henri Matisse's *The Conversation* except that through this window is seen a white mission station nestled in the arm of a malachite-green valley. The white has the luminosity of bleached shells.

In the foreground stand two guide dogs and to the left, in the corner, are propped two white canes.

Chapter 7

I meet Raphael downstairs and he asks me where Mossie is. I scream: Oh my God, Mossie! And I remember I told her to wait in the Bead Shop. Now the thing about Mossie is she doesn't think like us. So if I tell her to stay in the Bead Shop and don't move till I come back, she'll stay there till kingdom come.

Raphael and I run down Long Street. The Bead Shop's locked and everyone has gone home. We peer through the window into the already darkening shop and bang on it hard: Mossie! Are you in there? Mossie! Mossie!

There she is! Man, sometimes she makes me sick! She's sitting under one of the bead tables, twisting a finger through her hair. Can you believe that? How the hell are we going to get her out?

Raphael tries to force the lock with his knife but can't break it open. I find a brick round the side alley and throw it through the glass of the door. We kick at the shards and help Mossie through. She starts freaking out, waving her arms and jumping around while the alarm shrills through the air.

Raphael urges Mossie to hurry, pulling her by the arm as we bolt up Orphan Lane to get out of Long Street. I run alongside and scream so she nearly falls over her feet: Cops! Mossie, run!

She starts crying and shows me that she's scared of

jail. Her teacher told her that in prison, which is where she thinks Mossie is heading, you just get bread and water.

Raphael shouts at me to stop teasing her, but I'm angry and carry on: Jail's nice, Mossie! You won't have to go to school! All you do is watch videos!

Back in the flat our hearts beat hard. I make Mossie some tea and stir in six sugars. She shoves me in the stomach and wants to know why I said the police were behind us.

I pour her another cup of tea and say: Joke, Mossie. Can't you take a joke? She shakes her head hard and waves her arms around because she wants me to say sorry. I tell her she's the one who should say sorry.

She kicks the floor then looks at me sideways and starts to laugh.

This painting, called *She is the Little Sister*, is of a girl standing in the corner of a room. Her hands are clasped in front of her, her head tilted slightly to one side, her eyes soft and questioning.

Her shadow is smudged up against the wall, and we imagine the artist dipping his thumb into hadedah-silver-grey and with it fixing the shadow to the canvas.

One notices the borrowings from Amedeo Modigliani's *Little Girl in Blue*.

The staccato brushstrokes are carefree. The colours are wistful, like the softened yellow-grey-green of a baobab's fruit.

The frame is made of pigeon feathers and coloured beads pasted onto cardboard.

Chapter 8

Bernard lives on the fourth floor. He lives alone and has no friends except us. He sells flags at the Buitengracht intersection and dresses really well in designer suits and wide-brimmed hats. He comes from Mozambique and speaks Portuguese and rolling, round English.

We make friends because he is lonely, but he doesn't really want any friends. He often hangs out on the roof and that's where we mostly meet him. He is here illegally but we are the only ones who know and we would never tell anyone. He bought a passport from someone who works at Home Affairs and one of the Nigerians on the top floor sold him an ID. Both have legitimate serial numbers and Bernard's photos. The passport says he was born in Cofimvaba, though he was really born near Vila de Manica in Mozambique and his name was once Bernadino.

He will never return to Mozambique. Even though the war is over, he has no home to go back to and he does not know whether his wife and children are still alive.

We are sitting on the roof on flattened-out cardboard boxes watching the clouds which are full of rain but not yet raining and he says: *Surely this is so beautiful, the sky. I am thinking about the sky at my home, before the rain coming. I am thinking about the smell onto the ground when the rain starting to fall and those many, many ants flying out. You know those ants? They getting the wings just that one day to fly that one time. That smell of rain, it so sweet.*

It is the first time he has said anything about Mozambique. We say nothing as he tells us about his life before the war.

He worked in the villa of a rich landowner called Senhor Filipe de Oliveira. The Senhor had a beautiful wife called Senhora Sofia Isabel de Oliveira. Bernard's job was to carry water up from the reservoir and pour it into a ceramic water filter in the kitchen. The water slowly worked its way through layers of sand and charcoal and came out clear and cool. Bernard helped the cook and the houseboy. He polished the tiled floors, the brass and the silver, and served at table.

Every Friday Bernard helped Senhora Sofia Isabel de Oliveira hand out rations to the farm labourers and house staff. He opened large Hessian and cotton sacks in the dark storeroom. The workers lined up with three tins each. Into these Bernard poured a tin measure of flour, a tin measure of tiny, dried, kapenta fish and a tin measure of maize bits. If he dropped just one kapenta, someone would pick it up without being seen.

Senhora Sofia Isabel de Oliveira waved at the flies which flew about and patted her sweating neck with a white, lace handkerchief. She watched Bernard hand out the rations in the cool, dark storeroom at the side of the tobacco sorting shed. Inside, it smelt of Hessian and dryness. She nodded to each of the workers as they thanked her. She lowered her eyes to the ground without looking at their hard, bare feet and dusty, dry legs, then looked up again at the next worker, but looking past and beyond so she never saw the story in anyone's eyes.

When Bernard had finished handing out the rations, he locked the storeroom and gave her the key. Then he walked back with her, behind her, silently, to the kitchen of her villa or into the gardens, waiting for her to tell him what she wished to be done. And he noticed always her black hair piled up on her proud head and the straightness of her walk.

Once, after he had finished handing out rations, she gave him two empty, cotton meal-bags. He folded them up and took them home to his wife and she sewed them up into a dress for herself.

The picture, titled *It is the Senhora*, is of a dark-haired, aristocratic woman sitting on a chair intricately fashioned in wood, leather and brass. Her hunting dog dozes at her feet.

In the right-hand corner stands a man with an arrogant, upright posture holding a whip, wearing a black shirt with trousers tucked into knee-length boots.

In the left-hand corner sits a cardinal. His crimson robe covers an obesity which the rolls of his chin and paunched cheeks describe. At his feet lies an empty bottle of Madeira wine.

Hibiscus reds with source-of-the-Nile greens and blues express the seductive elegance of this painting.

We are reminded, particularly by the technique and choice of colour, of *Madame Matisse, Portrait with a Green Stripe*, by Henri Matisse. Perhaps too by the expression in the woman's eyes.

The frame is fashioned in corrugated card, spray-painted in gold.

Chapter 9

The Senhora Sofia Isabel de Oliveira, she a lonely lady. So because I work in the house I not to be looking at anything but I see everything. I see my Senhora sit against the window and crying. But I not to ask about the troubles. Only I know the Senhora lonely because all the sons they been sent to the war in Angola, and maybe they not come back one day. And my Senhor, he pay a lot of money to the Portugal government for his sons not be gone to the war in Angola. But all the sons they must go to the war. Then he see the war it starting in Mozambique too. The war coming to everywhere. The songs for the war they already arriving and the people they already got troubles.

Was she a nice lady, Bernard? The Senhora Sofia Isabel de Oliveira? (I like the sound of her name.)

I don't know to say she be a nice lady. She be a beautiful lady. Always she wear the beautiful clothes and the high shoes. But she not be talking to me. Only to tell me do this or do something. Sometimes I see her, she sit at the window with some sorrows. And sometimes I see her, she stand near to the wall also with some sorrows. But she be more kind than the Senhor. The Senhor, he be a difficult man and I never trying to make him be angry.

My wife, she also be working for the Senhor. She working with the tobacco. He got the big shed for dry the tobacco. My wife sort the tobacco. It be too hot inside and my wife sick many times from that smell of the tobacco and the hot inside that shed. Many people working the tobacco. But me, I working in the house. I working for my Senhora.

Big drops fall from the sky. They are so nice and cold that we don't go in. Mossie jumps up and runs around. She wants to get wet. Bernard lights a cigarette, picks a bit of tobacco off his tongue and tilts his panama hat slightly.

You know my job in the night? I light the gas for the lamps inside. And I serving the food to the Senhor and the Senhora. I wearing a white shirt and a white pants and I carry the food to the table in the silver plates. I not to spill or dropping anything. I got the white cloth on my arm and I pouring the red wine. They not talking to each other. I to stand still near to the table and they take the food. I stand there to wait they want something. They not saying anything. Only they just eat. When they finish to eat, they sit on the big chairs and I to bring the coffee. Still they not talking, they just drinking the coffee. Then the Senhora, she go to her room and I know she be crying. And the Senhor, he stay up the whole night and he smoke the cigarettes and the cigars and reading the books. Me, I to clear the table and washing the plates. Then I to wait for the Senhor to go sleep. And I put out the gas and then I go to my wife and childrens.

My Senhor, he got another woman to love in the town. Then sometimes he go into the town at night and my Senhora, she sit alone at the table. And I standing there to wait for her to eat the food. I pour the wine for her and I see she be too lonely. But I not to be talking to her, only to standing there to wait she want something. She finish the food, then she walking up and down the whole night. She walking up and down the house and maybe she crying but I not to be saying something. And when she hearing the truck to come and the Senhor he come back from the woman he love in the town, then my Senhora she go to her bed and she close the door. Then I to make the coffee for the Senhor and wait he finish to smoke the cigar and go to his bedroom. Then I putting out the gas and I go to the compound to my wife and childrens.

It starts to rain hard, so we all go inside.

I run a bath for Mossie and throw in her rubber duck and plastic bakkies to keep her busy: Don't wet your hair. You hear me? And use the soap, here. And don't get it in your eyes.

Our mother is closed up in her room. Raphael makes some coffee. Bernard is in talk mode.

How come you're remembering all this now, Bernard? I ask him. I thought you forgot everything.

Except for the reds and whites which leap out from this picture of a tavern, the colours are muted and subdued. The image is softened by the dim light of oil lamps.

A landowner, wearing tight, black pants tucked into high riding boots, leans his body against a young woman at the bar. His knee presses her legs apart, holding them open. His thigh is heavy against her, pressing her against the counter. Hanging beside him, as if in mid-air, is a coiled leather whip. On the bar are lined up empty bottles of wine and Laurentina beer.

The blood-red taffeta of the woman's full skirt is as seductive as the colour of roses. Her white breasts reflect the wild lilies which grow in the swamps nearby and which we glimpse, under moonlight, through an open window on the right.

Our thoughts turn, only because of the way the luminous texture of the cloth has been captured, to *Four Dancers* by Edgar Degas. There is also a sensuality in the woman's skin, similar to that shown by Degas's figures.

This work is called *It is the Cantina of Vila de Manica*.

Chapter 10

I also thinking I forget everything but today I remembering. I tell you something — you never to take a cigar from the Senhor. He can beat you for that. So you not walking again when he finish to beat you. Me, I never to take anything from his house. I not even take the food he leave on the plates. This I giving out to the pigs and those chickens.

That one who work before me, that José, he taking the cigar one time. The Senhor make him be tied on the tree and the boss-boy on the farm he to beat José. The Senhor he sit straight up on that big white horse and the horse it dig with the foot and it lift the head up and down, up and down because it an angry horse. It want only to run. But the Senhor he hold it tight to obey so he can watch the boss-boy to beat José.

The boss-boy beating José with the leather whip. So José, his whole back be open up with that whip and his wife come later to take him away because he not walk. Only he crying. And because his whole back open up and he got no doctor, he lie there with fever and he die after those few days. So you must all know that, never to take the cigar from my Senhor. Not even the half-finish cigar because maybe he want it later.

He breathes hard, takes a yellow hanky out of his top pocket and wipes his face.

This place I working for my Senhor, it a big farm and all the land, it belong to the Senhor. He got the cows and many fields. When the war starting many soldiers coming. One time Frelimo soldiers they coming. One time the soldiers from the

Ian Smith Rhodesia army they coming. Another time those Renamo soldiers, they also come. The people too afraid about those soldiers. This soldiers he tell you one thing. This other soldiers he tell you another thing. The people too afraid. Really.

He stops talking, drinks his coffee, puts his hat on, feels the knot of his tie and says: *I think I not to be remembering anymore. I say goodnight now.*

He hesitates at the door, turns back into the kitchen, looking down at the floor, one hand in his jacket pocket. Then he sits at the kitchen table and lights a cigarette.

Wait. I to tell you something about this soldiers. Whatever the soldiers, whatever the army they coming from, they got the same thing in the eyes. They got in the eyes something so when they look at you maybe you know you be the dead man soon. It better you look at the feet than look at the eyes of that soldier. But if you look at the feet, the soldier can shout at you to come here. And he can put his gun inside your mouth and asking you what you hiding inside your roof. And where you hiding that one from the other army? And where you hiding your maize? And all these things he asking so you are shaking your whole body and your teeth hitting against that piece of gun in your mouth. And that soldier he can say something about you to playing the music with your teeth on his gun and now you must dance. He can shoot around the feet so you jumping and all the other soldiers they laughing. Then he can kill you anyway.

This I telling you about the soldiers, what is all the same about all the soldiers, they all killing you anyway. You give them the maize, you show them where is the water, you try to deciding where is the other army hiding and you tell this soldiers. But they kill you anyway. When you see that eyes of the soldiers, you must just know you are soon dead. So what I telling you is this. When you see the soldiers mad from killing coming to your place, you better to hide away. No good try to talk with soldiers.

He wipes his face. Raphael also has to leave and they go out together.

I get Mossie out of the bath: I told you not to wet your hair, you rubbish. And stop laughing. It's not funny. How am I supposed to dry it? Well, you must just handle it.

I leave her to dry herself. I sit on the veranda and look out over the city. I wish I could write something about the way the full moon rises, yellow, over the high buildings; how it glides up silently from behind the forlorn office blocks. But I can't.

Instead I feel the hot breath of war puff into my face and make my eyes sting with the ash of burning villages; ash from the burning of thatched roofs; ash from the torched corn stores. War has crept in on its belly through the long grasses of the dry season and crossed the dry riverbeds to come close, close to me here in the city where bush war should not reach. War wants me to see that it is more powerful than anything good, and that it cannot be held at bay by non-war. Non-war is just a butterfly or soft petals. Strong wind or beating sun shrivels it.

But war, war howls with the *taka-taka-taka* of machine-gun fire tearing up the edges where sunset meets night; tearing up the curtain behind which life is supposed to be safe. It is the numberless refugees marching down like a column of ants to reach Skyline and safety. It is Bernard's untold nightmare. It is the terrible stories unfolding next to a steaming enamel teapot and thick slices of baked maize bread in Princess's flat.

Princess told me that she has a box of ammunition in her room. You must always keep weapons under your bed or buried at the edge of your village. You must always be ready. You must be ready to run, ready to leave everything behind and run, without shoes on your feet, through the jungles and through the burning sands. You must be ready also to die. Because bullets are a shower of rain and when they fall they always hit something.

But worse than this. You must be ready to kill your daughters, your girl children. Because when soldiers and rebels pour into a village they give a terrible death to your daughters. But you, you the mother, should hold your girls close to your breast and kill them in a gentle manner, before the soldiers touch them. Like Princess should have done.

The untitled tenth image captures the texture of an inner wall in a tobacco-sorting shed. One sees the roughness of limewash on unplastered brickwork, with the khaki-yellow mottling of fine tobacco dust flecked across it.

In the foreground stands a thin, black woman wearing a worn, floral print, cotton dress. The flowers on her dress are faded such that they have a sorrow about them, as if the garment has been washed at the river's edge, scrubbed on rocks and left to dry in the hot sun, many times.

She has tied a white, cotton meal-bag around her head as a turban.

We see her, among many other women, standing at a sorting table which is piled with large, dry tobacco leaves. The artist, in making this woman the emotional centre of the picture, lifts her face to look at the viewer. She looks out from the painting with a tender dignity similar to that of Giotto's Madonna in *Madonna and Child*.

The other women look down at the tobacco leaves they are sorting. Despite their anonymity the artist captures their fatigue and we imagine from their tired postures that they have known no life but this.

(The artist, in an early commentary, indicated that the woman portrayed here as the main subject was so poor that at the market-place she would gather up single grains of rice spilt by the merchants.)

Chapter 11

Months go by and she doesn't wake up in the night. She just takes her pills and goes to bed. Even when Raphael and Bernard are here drinking coffee, she doesn't wake up.

I'm lying on my bed in the glow. The door's closed and I'm listening to Counting Crows. Something wakes her up. I don't know what because it's really not me or Mossie. She's banging at our door and screaming: *Open this door! Open this door!*

Mossie just lies there. She's not asleep.

I shout that the door's open: The door's not locked! What do you want? Just come in!

Bang! Bang! Bang! Her hands are smacking against the door. It flies open. I can't see properly in the half dark. I just see her fly over to me, across the room, like a spook. She flies over and starts hitting me. *Bash! Bash! Bash!* On my face, my head, all over. I push at her, push her from me. Go away! Go away! Leave me alone! She falls down and I see she's not properly awake and I have to drag her again. I drag her to her bed. My face is throbbing. I'm shaking. I hate her.

When I've got her into bed I phone Raphael: Come fetch me, just come fetch me. Come now, please.

I don't take Mossie. I leave her in bed and tell her to stay there, go to sleep. Her eyes are screwed shut but I know from her breathing she's awake. One day

I must tell her that when she's really asleep her eyes don't screw up – they just shut.

Raphael catches a Rikki taxi and meets me down below. I don't have to say anything because he understands everything. I'm shaking from the cold but it's not cold. We walk to his house, up Orange Street, all the way up with the traffic going by. The traffic is groaning. The traffic is tired and pulling its way up towards the highway.

We pass the Labia where *Pillow Book* is showing and I go in to use the toilet. I look at myself in the mirror for a long time. I look at myself and think about who I am and about being in my body. I am the person inside this body, behind the face which is looking back at me from the mirror. How did I enter? How did I become this person? If I was not me inside this body would I be someone else, some other time, some other place? I tilt my head backward and then sideways. I shake my head and my hair waves about. How would I leave this time and place?

When I come out, Raphael is sitting on the pavement waiting for me. We walk up slowly to his house. The lounge is softly lit by one lamp and we sit there a long time. He plaits and unplaits my hair, then makes hot chocolate and we eat biscuits.

We sleep together in his bed. I want to live with him forever. He holds me so I feel his breath against me the whole night. His breath is warm and it deepens as he falls asleep. I lie against him and his arms tighten around me every time I move.

We wake up early before the sun has risen. I don't want his mother to know what happened. He holds me and kisses my mouth, open. His body is warm and mine feels so cold. I like this closeness, this touching. I like him to touch me, touch my face, my hair. I close my eyes.

Raphael gets dressed to walk back with me but I say: No. No, it's okay. No, I'm fine now. I'll see you at school, later. I run home in the sharp air. There's less traffic now but soon, when the day begins, it will start roaring again, like lava pouring from a volcano.

And as I run, I think of him and his beautiful eyes and the way he looks at me sometimes. He is my only friend outside Skyline. We are very close, even though the only things we have in common are that we don't have fathers and don't hang out in groups. We became friends the first time we met. We just sat on a wall at break, talking.

Raphael told me how his grandparents survived Nazi persecution in Holland and how they came to South Africa after the war. He told me how they got rich selling furniture; how his father drowned when they all went boating one summer; how his mother lives her whole life through him because he is her only child and she has no one else. Raphael can't remember his father. I didn't tell Raphael anything about my family. He just found out everything because since that day, when we first made friends, we've done most things together.

As I reach home the silver voice of the muezzin calls from the mosque in Loop Street. Our mother is in the kitchen. She doesn't look at me and acts like nothing happened. I wish she was dead.

Mossie is lying in bed, awake, the blanket pulled over her head. I pull it off her. Have you been crying, Mossie? What you been crying for? I just went out. You know I always come back. Last night? Just a dream, Mossie. A bad dream. Come, you'll miss the bus.

I help her dress and brush her hair a bit, but it's full of knots because she's been twisting it, so I just do the top. We walk down the stairs slowly because it won't really matter if she misses the bus, we'll just cruise down Long Street. I'm not in a rush today. There's nothing I'm feeling good about.

Downstairs in the foyer some kids from the sixth floor say something smart about Mossie and start laughing. I rush them. I grab the one by the throat and ram him against the wall: You got something wise to say about my sister? You got a problem because she can't talk right? You little shit! You got a problem? Hey? Hey? I'm screaming. I've lost it. I start to smash him but his brothers grab my arms and throw me down. They grab me and try to push me out of the foyer but I kick at them and they leave me.

Mossie starts freaking out and my head is bursting. Shut up! Leave me some space, Mossie. Shit! Can't you see I need space? Space! Understand? I shake her and don't care that she's crying. Somehow I get her on the bus and walk to school.

Now we're all here in English and this prick of a teacher's trying to tell me something I already know about. So I look wise and say something wise and he tells me to get out of the class. So I just walk home. Where do they find these morons who run schools? And walking home I wonder if Raphael will always be my friend.

You think that boy will stay with you? Our mother once asked me. *His mother knows your type. She won't let him stay with you. He's just having a good time. You wait and see. A good Jewish boy like him, what's he want with someone like you? Just good times for a while, then he'll drop you. Mark my words!*

I wait for Mossie's bus. She takes my hand to cross the road. She pulls me to stop on the pavement and makes me understand that she knows I want space. And I can have all the space I want. She spreads out her arms and turns around: All the space I want. Her mouth is open wide and laughing and her eyes are all screwed up. She hugs me. I give her a shove.

Later we take empty bottles down to Okkie Blomdal on the corner. His shop stinks. The walls are plastered with pictures of naked girls and one of Mao Tse-tung. He wants to know: *You buy these Cokes here?*

Sure, sure we buy these Cokes here, you old stinker.

He throws the deposit money across the counter to us. His bottom denture slips forward and he sucks up spit.

We go over to 7Eleven to buy sweets and old bread. Then I take Mossie down to the Gardens to feed the squirrels.

In this painting, *She Has More Sorrow in the Kitchen,* developed from the earlier charcoal work, *She Has Sorrow in the Kitchen,* a woman sits leaning on a Formica-topped table. The artist has allowed a theme of tragic loneliness to develop in these two works.

The woman holds her hands together, level with her left cheek. From the fingers of one hand dangles a cigarette, the ash grown long. A single, bright bulb makes everything stark.

In the background we see a window, hung with blue-checked calico.

A pot of purple violets stands on the window sill together with a bottle of Sunlight liquid. There is also a cup of water, without a handle, in which a single violet leaf has taken root.

The woman's eyes and her posture are so sad that to look at this picture makes the viewer forget about hope.

One reflects on the similar tragic figure of Edgar Degas's *Absinthe.*

Chapter 12

Okkie Blomdal's shop is full of empty bottles. He pays out deposits but never calls the bottle company to collect the empties.

He's into his bottles in a big way. There are millions of them in his shop. Not just Coke bottles, because if you go there late in the day he'll pay you a deposit for any kind you bring in.

I don't know how to describe his place. We're talking about a bottle graveyard here. Every kind of bottle in the world ends up in these stockpiles, covered in dust, full of cobwebs and spiders. Even the small yard at the back is stacked to the sky with empties.

Okkie Blomdal was a mercenary and fought in most of the wars up Africa – the Belgian Congo, Rhodesia, Angola. He fought on whichever side paid him the most. He took payment in whatever form it came – money, raw gold, diamonds. In the Congo he followed in the wake of fleeing colonists and swaggered into homes which people had abandoned in mid-meal. He and his group of soldiers pushed forward with their bayonets, drinking and plundering. They killed anything which whimpered or moved and they took whole table-loads of silverware, tied up in tablecloths and slung over their shoulders.

When he fought in Angola he changed sides as it suited him, Unita and the South African army in the wet months and the MPLA in the dry months. He helped shoot up the migrating herds of elephants which flowed across the Caprivi Strip like a river. This is how he came to make a fortune of money – with ivory.

Now he is just a disgusting and crazy old man. He stinks and can't keep half a thought going. He wears his hair in a long, greasy, grey ponytail and his eyes are sunk deep in his head. Veins throb at his temples and he spits at people when he's angry. He rolls dagga and is always puffing on a joint. Under his bed he keeps his fortune of banknotes stuffed in suitcases. It is the only place he doesn't keep bottles.

I get into bed before our mother comes home. I don't want to see her. I've been asleep a long time when screeching cats wake me up, late in the night. But it's not cats, it's sirens. Blue lights are flashing, flashing, flashing. I rush to the veranda. There's an ambulance and police and a small crowd outside. I see them load a stretcher into the ambulance. The body is covered.

Next morning Sylvester from 7Eleven tells us that Okkie Blomdal was murdered in the night.

I told him someone would come one day. Well, now they did. He put up a fight, oh ja. With his bayonet. You know that old bayonet he had on the wall? That's what he tried to kill them with.

He bends over laughing.

Can you just see that? The old bugger stabbing away with his bayonet at those Congo fighters!

He stands in Rambo mode and stabs at the air, then bends over laughing again, hitting his thighs.

Anyway, he'd never match a whole pack of those illegals. They come with their guns and you haven't got a hope in hell. You know what I mean? Man, there was blood everywhere, even in the bottles. And you know? There was so much money under the bed, they couldn't even carry it all! There was bundles of notes all over the place. It's true, I'm telling you. And you know? They didn't even run. Just killed him, took the money and walked out cool as cool.

They know Mr Mandela's justice has gone to shit. They just got to come down from Africa and take over our country. Fuck up their own place, then come here to steal from us. I'm telling you, the old days was better. Those apartheid days, you can give them back to me anytime. At least in those days, there was electric fences around the border and if illegals came over they fried on the wires. These guys couldn't just stroll across like now. Know what I mean?

And also, with apartheid, you kill someone and they hang you. You swing, man. Now nobody swings. The country's just gone to shit. It belongs to illegals now, not us. They bought it! They paid somebody something under the counter. I'm telling you! South Africa belongs to Africa, not us.

I'm not into blacks, you know that, hey? But at least our blacks are better than those others. They're just dangerous, man.

And you know? He points at me. *I see you always hanging round with that black guy who sells the flags. You watch your step with him. Blacks are all the same. They're all thieves. Sleep with dogs, you get fleas. Know what I mean?*

I tell him he's talking shit.

The police board up Okkie Blomdal's shop for the investigation. But someone busts open the side window and almost overnight all the bottles go. People want to know how so many bottles can just evaporate into thin air. Who the hell wants bottles?

The bergies, that's who! Fucking hotnots, says know-all Sylvester from 7Eleven. *That's why we haven't seen any of them around these past few days. Who's seen a bergie around here, hey? Tell me, who's seen a hotnot around here?* He asks no one in particular.

They came like rats over a carcass and cleaned up the old crazy's shop. Every last bottle! One minute his shop's full of bottles. The next minute the whole lot's gone. Not even a chip of glass left! Fucking hell! The country's gone to shit, I'm telling you! Illegals take his money! Bergies take his bottles!

On Sunday morning Raphael and me and Mossie lean against the wall, just passing time. Chris and Adelaide, two of the bergies who hang around here, push their trolley up to us. Adelaide hands Mossie a doll with one arm they found in someone's rubbish. *You like the dollie, missie? No, missie, you must hold it! That's why I brought it to you! To keep! Ag, shame! I will find you the arm. Don't worry, missie!*

Mossie doesn't like dolls, so she gives it to Gracie later when we go upstairs. Gracie scrubs it, ties a scarf around it like a sarong, sprays it with cologne and props it up on the bathroom window ledge.

Raphael asks Chris where all the bottles are and whether they have gone to the recycling depot already, all sold, all turned into money and drink.

Bottles? No master, I never saw no bottles. Really, master. We only collect newspaper and card. Not bottles. You know us, hey master?

Chris and Adelaide smell bad. They drink meths now, so their eyes shimmer and push everything towards darkness, letting in only the tiniest streaks of light.

They keep all their things down a manhole and sleep at the end of the lane on the side of Kennedy's Cigar Bar. If it's raining or cold they sleep in doorways, never at the homeless shelter because then they can't be together.

Ag, you know missie, says Adelaide, *I'm sleeping with my Chris now so long. How can they ask me to sleep on my ownsome? And you know, you can't even take a little dop in with you. It's the same like in jail. You must go in dry and come out dry and that's hard. I don't take a lot of drink, you know that, hey missie? But a little dop in the night. Ag, that's so good. So me and Chris, we rather sleep in the street. Then we can be together and have our dop and keep each other cozy, you see?*

In this, the untitled twelfth picture, a black, probably homeless woman sits on the pavement outside Rebel Liquor bottle store. Behind her a poster advertises a weekend special on Southern Comfort.

The woman's back is bent as she leans forward slightly, one arm balanced on a knee, the hand hanging limp.

She wears a doek around her head, tied low at her neck.

Her skin is dry and weathered, her teeth yellow. She tilts her head slightly, and we see in her the same weariness of spirit as captured by Paul Cezanne in his *The Negro Scipio*.

In the background stands a supermarket trolley piled high with newspapers.

We see the back view of a white woman entering the bottle store, a long plait curving on her back like a serpent.

Chapter 13

I listen to the wind. It's growling like something wild and with its own life. Everyone here hates the wind because it whistles down the stairwell and whines under doors and windows. Cliff and Gracie get lost in it. It hammers at them so they can't walk straight and soon lose their bearings.

Sometimes the wind howls like many splintered words around me. And the words call out: *Make of us poems and ballads. Make of us sweet stories of delight.*

And sometimes the concrete masonry and verandas of Skyline line up like lonely letterings and they cry to me: *Form us. Form us into song. Fashion of us tales and tellings that we may have some meaning. Weave of us literature so that we may become something worthy.*

And the traffic will twist and turn in anguish wanting the flowings of a fine composition.

Or the people here, the newly arrived, the sad and broken people, will line up in front of me, looking out from behind torn garments and the dusty dreams of Africa and they will whisper: *Turn our desolation into something memorable. That it may not have been in vain to lose what little we owned. Make for our lost children a chime of gentle sound that they might follow it and escape, one day, from the plateau of war.*

And those who have triumphed after their long march, those who have turned their backs on what they left behind and built a new life here at the top of Long Street, they ask only a love sonnet to be whispered in the late night for the beloved who was buried with the countless others.

So I gather up the words which I find spewed across the tar of Long Street and at the foot of Skyline and I try to turn them into poetry. I try to re-embroider these splintered words into the finery they once were – old litanies from Ethiopia; chantings from Sudan; fables from Eritrea. But I cannot turn the city's laments into anything of beauty.

An old man lies outside Long Street Baths. But he's not really old. His hair is stringy and dirty and his denims are torn. His shoes are old and bashed and he has no socks. He has wet himself and the puddle underneath him runs down the pavement.

I see him around often, always looking for drink, holding up a piece of cardboard which says: *Homeless. Please give your small change.*

It should say: *I am Charles. I sleep in the outside toilet of my ex-brother-in-law's house. I've been to Angola and back again. I think I helped shoot up hundreds of blacks. If I don't have a drink I go crazy listening to them babble from a mass grave.*

I get a disability pension and a small army pension but it's not enough. I need thirty rand a day for drink so I don't hear the babbling. You are quite right, I'm going to drink myself to death. The meths is all I can get now. I don't waste time straining the purple dye out through bread. I just drink it. If I don't get a drink I have to claw at the grave to get those bodies out.

General Malan! General Malan! General Magnus Malan! Give me a drink, man! Or help me dig up this grave! Free these dead blacks, man! I didn't want to kill them! I was just a kid! Following your orders. You never told me why I was going to Angola. I just got my call-up papers and got in the truck with the other conscripts and off we went. Off we went into fucking hell and back again.

Words fly off him and glow as cinders against the cityscape.

One day I will leave Skyline and live with Mossie in a nice house up on the side of the mountain. Then I'll find words in places other than wind and war and traffic. I will find beauty and words of a new order.

At school the principal says they are all complaining about me, all the teachers, and he wants to see my father. I tell him my father is dead.

This untitled water colour is not framed. It is torn and flimsy, and one senses the artist would like the wind to blow it away.

It is of a white vagrant, sitting on his haunches outside Kentucky Fried Chicken.

He holds his worn-out hat in his hands and this gives him an air of supplication.

He has a half-filled bottle of purple meths in his jacket pocket.

His eyes have nothing in them but a plea, captured by a translucent dove-grey.

The background is worked in the smudgy blue-grey of rain-laden clouds; the foreground in muddy creams.

A white woman stares at the pavement as she strides onto the canvas from the right. She is thin with a long plait draped over her shoulder.

Pinned on the wall behind the vagrant is a bright yellow and blue election poster: *The Guts to Fight Back. Vote DP.*

Chapter 14

I ask Bernard about his children but he is afraid to talk about them. Why are you afraid? I want to know.

Only I afraid because I not knowing what happen to them. When the soldiers they come to us, they shoot Senhor de Oliveira and they shoot also the Senhora. And they come for us in the kitchen and they make us to stand against the wall and to watching the Senhora die on the floor. I see the blood coming from her ears. Her eyes look a little at me and her hand it moving a little to reach me and then her eyes looking nowhere.

The soldiers they say these be bad people, these Senhor who owning the farm. They take all the money and guns of the Senhor and the silver candles and all the silver plates. Everything of the silver they take. The soldiers take off the rings and the gold from the arms of my Senhora. But the rings not coming off from her fingers, so the soldier he just chop down with his knife. That soldier he make me pick up the fingers of my Senhora and take the rings for him, then he make me to throw the fingers outside to the ground. These the fingers of my Senhora.

Then they take all our childrens. All the childrens they take them. They want our childrens to be the soldiers so we never to see our childrens again. My wife she crying and all of the mothers working on the Senhor's farm they crying for these childrens. But the soldiers hit the mothers and steal all the childrens. I running after to fetch my children back, but the soldiers they shooting me and I falling over and I think I be dead. I never to see my childrens again.

We are on the roof. He closes his eyes. His hands are trembling. He sings softly in Portuguese:

Como um inútil rio seco,
Do qual ninguém levanta água,
Meu coração com tristeza torna-se pó seco,
Tem uma mágoa só sua.[1]

Shall I get us some chips, Bernard? He nods: *Yes, I thinking that be fine idea.*

He gives me some money. I tell Mossie to stay there with him and I race down the stairs. I don't wait for the lift. I buy two packets of hot chips from Mr Texi's Fish Shop and spread them out on paper in front of us. But Bernard just looks at them and my stomach turns a bit, so I also don't feel like eating them. Mossie eats them all because they taste nice, all salty with vinegar.

Near to the farm there be the mission of the Sisters of Mercy. So they fixing my arm where the soldiers shooting me. And many peoples hiding there inside the church. But the soldiers they coming there too. They kill the Sisters of Mercy and they put fire to the church and the mission house and many peoples there they stuck inside the church and they burning. They not to get out because the soldiers they locking that door. And we hear those peoples screaming inside the fire.

---

[1]Like a uselessly dried-out river,
Which no one lifts water from,
My heart with sadness has become dry dust,
It has a sorrow all its own.

Only the birds they get away from the fire. Those the black birds sitting on the roof, they fly when the fire burning. We running away and all we seeing behind us is that fire and those black birds flying. So the Sisters of Mercy they be killed and many of the peoples hiding there, they also be killed. But some, we running away.

My wife she cannot run nicely. My wife she shouting, she crying always about those our childrens. She stopping all the time and I pulling her to come. The soldiers burning everything and we must run quickly. But then I losing my wife. I not understand how I losing my wife because I think we running together but then I see she not with me. And I not knowing if she fall or she too tired to running anymore so maybe she just fall and not getting up again. But I not see that. I so sorry I not see my wife falling down and not running with me. Then I not know if those soldiers they shoot my wife because she looking back for our childrens.

Mossie is curled up with her head in my lap. Bernard is leaning against the wall. His eyes are closed.

You see this my fault. This my fault that I losing my wife. If I not losing my wife then we to finding our childrens. This is all to be my fault, this terrible thing. I not remember anything after. Maybe a little I remember of many more shooting and many more people to dying. But I not wanting to remember so I forgetting everything. I forgetting everything. Everything. I forgetting the names of my children. You see that terrible thing? I forgetting the names of my children.

He puts his face into his hands and his body shakes.

*What I remembering only is these soldiers, these army. These
army they not leave me. They to follow inside me. They find me
in the night-time. And you see, like today, they find me on the
roof here. They wanting me to die, these army. They to follow
inside me till they kill me.*

I don't know what to do. I push Mossie gently away
from me. She sits quietly, looks away. Rocks a bit.

I touch Bernard's back. I put my hand on his back
and run it down his spine. I run my hands down his
back and across his shoulders. His eyes are closed and
tears are running down his face. I want to say, don't
cry, Bernard. Bernard, your children are somewhere.
Bernard, I will help you find them. But I say nothing.
Because I know I can't do anything.

This fourteenth picture, worked in subdued greys and
mournful tones of iron and silver, is titled *It is the Death
of the Holy Mother under the Trees*. It depicts the mother
superior of a Catholic missionary order.

She has been stripped of her garments. Her head is
shaved. She tries to cover her body with her hands.

Blood pours from a wound on her head and this messy
scarlet in which we see slow, pensive and concentrated
brushwork is the only bright colour in the image.

Behind her the mission house burns and the naked
bodies of her holy sisters hang by their necks from the
branches of trees.

Across the background flies a flock of crows.

Chapter 15

The Spice Girls, Alice and Bluebell, live next door. They are not actually girls but men who cross-dress in silks and satins. They run hostess evenings in their flat and Alice also does cabaret shows at the Whistle Stop Café downstairs. Their flat is painted purple and has two huge, soft, double beds and a deep, white couch covered in cushions. The windows are draped with beautiful purple and pink curtains and they have shaggy, pink scatter-rugs thrown across their white carpets.

They always wear women's clothes – trendy things during the day, but at night, to work, they wear the most amazing, glittering, sequin-spangled dresses. They take hours to get ready and put on lots of make-up with long, false eyelashes and pencilled-in brows.

Alice and Bluebell have regular customers and a long waiting list, but because they only work at night I can leave Mossie there for hours during the day if I need to. They don't mind. If she ever can't go to school, like if she's sick, or it's her birthday and I don't want to stay with her, I take her to the Spice Girls and they look after her. Mossie hates going to school on her birthday because she has to wear a crown and stand on a chair while everyone sings 'Happy Birthday'. Bluebell tells her it's great to be a queen. But Mossie always works herself up into such a panic about it that I never force her to go.

Mossie loves the Spice Girls. They let her dig around in their cupboards and drawers which are full of dresses and scarves, wigs, make-up, fake jewellery and perfumes. They give her all their leftover make-up and do her face when she wants to play drag. Bluebell paints Mossie's face: *There, now close your eyes, sweetness,* and she colours her lids green, drawing black lines over her eyebrows.

Now make your lips like a big, fat kiss. That's it! Bluebell paints her mouth with ruby lipstick and covers Mossie's golden curls with a long, black Cleopatra wig. Bluebell shows her how to do a little strut with a quick, sexy turn, swishing her wig out, tilting her head down and looking up: *Sultry, lovie. Look sultry or you'll be wasting your time.*

Mossie totters around in a pink, satin kimono with huge sleeves which drag on the floor and oversized, high heels. *Now sweetie, just take it easy there!*

Later, down at Mr Texi's Fish Shop, we buy fresh fish for Raphael's mother. All along the counter dead fish are lined up with their eyes looking straight up at the flickering neon lights. Without the ocean their eyes seem like soft glass. I look at Raphael's mother's fish, the one we've chosen. I imagine the last thing it saw: a million silver brothers swimming alongside. I think about the ocean current running along with them, encouraging them towards the land mass and back out into the open ocean, playing with them.

The silver bodies are now lying on the ice in rows. *Thwack! Thwack!* Mr Texi chops off their heads and tails and tosses them into a bin behind him. Tails and heads and fins and scales pile up without the ocean, without the ocean waters. Our fish's eyes and the current of silver brothers it once swam with are frozen still in time, looking at us.

There's quite a crowd in the shop, waiting to be served. Alice the Spice Girl walks in and straight up to the counter with her bum out a little and her shoulders tight back so her fake breasts are high. She asks for two fish and chips.

You want some chips? She asks us over her shoulder. We don't, but she orders for us anyway: *And three hot chips, please.*

She's really beautiful, even from behind. She's wearing a tiny miniskirt with a tight top and platform sandals, so she looks even taller than she is.

Hey! Everybody! You think that's a woman?

Everyone turns round to see who's shouting his mouth off. There's Sylvester from 7Eleven pointing at Alice. I don't know why it's such a big deal for Sylvester and why he has to make such an issue.

Hey! Is that the new Mrs Texi? He shouts and everyone who works there tries not to laugh, but it's hard. Mr Texi is not into cross-dressing. He thinks the Spice Girls are disgusting and it's not a joke for him. He looks stern and his face is wet with sweat. But he doesn't say anything.

Alice won't turn round. She looks straight ahead at the great pans of bubbling oil waiting for her fish and chips. Sylvester's words hang in the oil-soaked air above the fry pans. But he can't let go and shouts again: *Hey! Check the new Mrs Texi!*

Alice takes her fish parcel, turns round gracefully and walks out, glancing around the shop. She is a great lady. As she passes him she says in a low voice: *Go fuck your face, Sylvester.*

She hands us our chips and leans down to hug Mossie. *You look gorgeous! Going someplace? Come back up later, I've got a new Janet Jackson. You like that? Sure, come over, okay?*

She blows a kiss across the shop.

In the fifteenth picture, *You Can Buy the Love Here*, a statuesque woman stands with one hand on her hip, the other pointing at the artist. The strength of her thighs is accentuated by an emerald-green, linen robe draped across them.

Thick curls tumble around her broad, masculine shoulders and her lips pout like a giant, red butterfly much like those of Dante Gabriel Rossetti's *Astarte Syriaca*.

The brooding and sensual confidence of this painting is captured by strong, commanding tones of olives and greens brushed towards and into flame-reds.

Chapter 16

The two things Mossie likes best in the world are beads and her roof birds. She doesn't like going to the New Horizons Care Centre because it's boring. Her teachers treat her in a really limited way because she has never shown them any of the amazing things she can do. They see her words get caught up and not form properly and watch her laugh at the wrong time and think she can't do things with her mind. They don't realize that she plays bridge and poker like an ace and that no one can beat her. She has never shown them how she loves and understands patterns and symmetry.

Mossie knows every bead in her collection and keeps them in jars next to her bed with her favourites on the window ledge. She sleeps with little jars of beads instead of teddies. Sometimes she goes to bed without pyjamas on and pours beads onto herself and all along the edge of her body. They make her feel warm inside herself and she lies dead still all through the night, covered in them.

I tell her she must go to New Horizons like I must go to school. That's just how it is and we've got no choice. When she's there she just turns her mind in, so it faces inside and not out. She always does this when something doesn't interest her so it looks like she's in a dream swaying and hugging herself.

I take her down to the Bead Shop most afternoons. The first time I took her in was a bad mistake because I really didn't know she'd get into beads in such a big way. We were walking back from town going up to meet Raphael and stopped at the Bead Shop window. Mossie pressed her face to the glass and I couldn't move her.

Okay Mossie, I said, when I realized this was interesting for her, we'll go in but don't touch anything.

Well, that was stupid, telling her not to touch. She moved from one table to another, stunned by what she saw: blue beads, yellow beads, glass beads, wooden beads, crystals, golds, spirals, rounds. Then she let out a squeal and started filling her pockets.

You know how time stretches sometimes? Well, time stretched then. It stretched long and slow. People in the shop stood rigid and no one moved. Everyone just stared at her. I watched the owner, Mrs Naidoo, glide over in slow motion with her cheeks puffing in and out and her hands ready to strangle Mossie.

Mossie doesn't understand about danger. Mrs Naidoo grabbed her and tried to release the fistfuls of beads but Mossie had found the possibility of new patterns in her life. The patterns were right there in the countless bits of colour and light. No one could move her. I tried very hard to get some sense into her but it was impossible. Usually I can, but I couldn't that day.

We were there until dark and eventually Mrs Naidoo called the police. Finally Mossie just got tired, lay down holding handfuls of beads and fell asleep. She looked like a sweet, smiling baby and one of the policemen carried her home.

Mrs Naidoo was really angry and said we could never, ever come into the shop again or cross to her side of the road or walk on her bit of pavement.

Next day I explained this to Mossie and she went into a serious decline. She waved her arms around and got angry and pointed down there, down Long Street, and made all her noises.

Of course, I knew what she was saying. She was telling me she had to go back to that shop but I pretended not to understand. What? You want a Coke at 7Eleven? Okay, let's go down. What? You want to swim at the Baths? Okay, let's go. But this just made her more and more frantic.

Finally one day she just didn't get out of bed. Nothing I could do got her up. She stayed in bed for days. I brought her all her favourite junk food: Marie biscuits spread with Marmite and jam; Coco Pops with Coke instead of milk; a Magnum ice cream. She didn't even look at them. Every time I tried to push her out of the bed she just stiffened her body, screwed her eyes shut tight and made her sound for those beautiful, coloured jewels down there in Long Street. I realized she was going to stay in bed until she died.

I got ten rand from Alice and went down to the Bead Shop. I held it up like a white flag and Mrs Naidoo shouted: *You! You get outta here! You get outta my shop! You hooligan! Get out! Rasheed! Call the police! Call the police! Rasheed!*

I said quietly, really quietly: Look, it's just me. I haven't brought my sister. I just want to buy some beads, not make trouble.

She glared at me and said: *Okay. But if you make any trouble Rasheed will throw you out. And Rasheed! Call the police anyway.*

I said to myself: Does she think I'm thick, or what? But to her, I just smiled. I bought ten little packets of ten different kinds of beads and took them home to Mossie.

She was sitting on the edge of the bed, all dressed and ready to go. I pushed her over and roughed her up a bit and said: How'd you know where I went, you rubbish? She hugged me and that was the end of staying in bed forever. She spent the next day sorting and mixing and getting a set of patterns in her mind. Then she came over to me with a serious face to let me know that she needed more. And that's how it all began.

First we had to convince Mrs Naidoo to let Mossie into her shop again. Raphael went in ahead of us and we waited at the door. He leaned on the counter looking smooth and put our money down. We'd got some from his mom and some from Bernard and we also sold Mossie's Bunnykins plate at Long Street Junk. This all came to R54.80. Raphael spread it out and said he wanted a selection of beads.

Mrs Naidoo said: *No, that's fine, just take a tray and choose what you want, then come up to me to pay.*

Raphael turned to the door and signalled to us to come in. Before coming here, we had tidied Mossie up so she looked very respectable. Not that she looked a mess before. It's just that I don't always brush her hair very well, especially when I'm in a hurry. And she does look quite grubby sometimes. On that day we made her look really squeaky-clean and pulled her hair back into a ponytail. Then we told her the Bead Shop rules: No squealing. No shouting. No jumping up and down. No fistfuls down your front. Nothing in your pockets except what you've paid for and what's been put in brown packets. Never, never make trouble with the owner. Otherwise no beads and no patterns. Mossie understands everything when she wants to. She stood there looking like Little Miss Goody Two-Shoes. Trouble was the last thing on her mind.

Rasheed! screamed Mrs Naidoo. *Rasheed!* But Raphael had already worked out that Rasheed is nobody. Rasheed is just a pretend security guard who never comes out from the back to throw you out.

Okay Rasheed! I'll deal with this. Okay you hooligans, you can buy some beads. But let me tell you this. If you steal one bead, if you steal just one bead, and believe me, I'll know because all the beads are on computer and see, (she pointed to a sign that said Protected by Tom and Gerry Security) *this shop has sur-vey-lance. Sur-vey-lance. You understand? I'll know when you're stealing and then you're finished! Finished!*

Raphael steered Mossie to the tables and she started to choose beads. She was as good as gold and concentrated very hard, without making a sound. We were there a long time. Eventually Raphael and me sat on the pavement outside breathing in Long Street traffic fumes and getting headaches. So we had to add another rule. We decided that Mossie could never be in there for more than half an hour except for special occasions. Like her birthday.

That night she couldn't go to sleep and stayed up very late sorting her beads. She begged to stay home from New Horizons the next day, so I took her and her beads to the Spice Girls for the morning. I knew she would just have got into trouble at school.

Alice and Bluebell *oohed* and *aahed* over her beads and when I fetched her after school I told her the last Bead Shop rule. Beads can only keep you home sometimes. New Horizons is important. Even if it's boring.

In this untitled painting, flat, open movements of translucent colour capture a sense of serenity and thoughtfulness. A young, barefoot girl sits on a window ledge overlooking a city.

She looks over her shoulder and we see her face in profile. Beside her on the window ledge is a vase of spring flowers. Around her neck hang cascades of beads.

Through the window we look down onto the red roofs of the city and far in the distance we see the harbour and outline of cranes.

Behind her, above the buildings and unseen by her, floats a white woman wearing a greatcoat, clutching a handbag and smoking a cigarette.

As with Marc Chagall's *Ida at the Window*, there is a tranquillity in this picture which compels the viewer to think about the girl's quiet thoughts and wonder why the woman is gazing at her.

Chapter 17

Mossie's second-best in the world are her roof birds. I take her up to the roof every day after school so she can change their water and put down food. She puts out bowls of bread chunks, sunflower seeds, birdseed, chopped-up leftovers, chopped-up vrot fruit from 7Eleven and water. Raphael buys her the seed from Atlas Trading and she keeps it in the storeroom near the washing lines, also on the roof.

In the beginning I didn't mind the birds, there were only about ten of them. But now there are close on a thousand coming down to eat. So there's lots of bird crap. Mainly pigeons and seagulls come to Mossie's roof restaurant, but she also feeds starlings and now and then white-eyes find their way here.

Mossie likes to keep all the birds under control. She wants the little birds to eat first, then the doves, then the pigeons. The seagulls have to eat last and they can polish off the leftovers. They don't like the system much and line up on the wall like soldiers waiting for a gap. She's got them all quite well trained now, but if she turns her back the seagulls move in with lots of agro and push their way to the best food.

I know you're not going to believe me, but I swear she knows every bird that she feeds. And the way she knows when a bead is missing she also knows when a bird is gone. They haven't got names or anything, they just make a pattern in her mind, so when one's missing, it's obvious to her. They all look the same to me.

Mossie's been waiting a long time for one of her birds to build a nest but none of them seem interested in roosting on the roof. She often leans over the edge looking across Cape Town, trying to figure out where all her birds' eggs are.

Bernard's up here on the roof, lying in the sun. I wait for Mossie to finish feeding her starlings. Some eat from her hands and she sways and laughs.

He has a terror again. He lies here on the roof to feel steady. War stalks him day and night, burning him, circling about him with dry flames of nightmare. He has nothing to still the terror with. He cannot shoot it down and can't pour water onto it. It is barbed wire around his heart and cryings in his mind. It is loss and it is unbearable.

I have fire inside. I have fire around me. Everything is fire for me. And I feel inside me when all those soldier boots coming, coming and the ground it crying and all the insects they stop to singing because the armies coming like those killing ants. You know those killing ants? They marching all together some hundreds and hundreds and everything they passing over they eat it and only bones they leaving behind. This is like those armies running through the land and shaking those fields. And they put down those small bombs so when you come to plough you can explode yourself and be dead, flying up to the sky, just some blood and pieces.

He lies in the sun with his legs and arms spread out and plays with his mind to make himself feel that he's falling into the blue sky. I lean against the wall watching him. Sweat beads sit across his lip. Beads of sweat and little rivers of sweat run down his face.

Bernard, are you okay? I ask him.

No, I not so okay. Nothing is so okay. I counts the dead all the time. I counts the bullets over and over. This is the fever inside me. When the armies come, I am young man. When the war is fighting, I am young man. When I run away over rivers, in the fevers, still I am young man. But now I grow old. My spirit grow old. I cannot to stop those armies. Still now they coming to my sleep and my dreaming and even they coming when it is daytime.

Bernard, can I get you something?

No, I not needing something. I just thinking maybe it better I die when my wife falling. Maybe I wrong to be the one who living now. Why I be the one to live and they all to die? I am such loneliness now. I am such loneliness now my wife is falling and my childrens gone. I cannot stopping the armies in my heart. But I try to be okay. I try.

He trembles.

Sometimes we help him sell flags. Sometimes when his hands shake we hold them.

His flat is bare. He has a portable radio, a sleeping mat, one pillow and two neatly folded blankets. All his clothes hang on wire coat-hangers off nails around the rooms: his shirts, jackets, ties and broad-brimmed hats.

There's nothing much in the kitchen. An aluminium teapot, a kettle, a few mugs and plates, a 1991 Total garage calendar stuck up on the wall. The bathroom is also bare. He likes good colognes and aftershaves and these line up along the edge of the bath.

Everything I got, it is before the war. I not got a many things in those days. I not a rich man in those times because I not got school, I not know the reading. I not got the money because my Senhor he pay only with food and to let us living on his land. My wife she grow some pumpkin and the vegetables. Only at the Christmas time my Senhor give us some money for that whole year. But I got my wife and my childrens. I got the nice children. I wish to show you one day these fine childrens. We got those songs to sing in the night when it is darkness. This all I have. But you see? It is on the other side. Before the war.

He sings:

A nossa canção de amor como laranjas inchadas,
Encanta o meu coração outra vez com toda a tua doçura,
Deixa-me tocar a tua face, os teus olhos negros.
Aonde está a tua voz líquida, aonde canta ela agora? [2]

I can't tell him he has got us, because one day me and Mossie are going to move from here to go live up where Raphael lives.

---

[2] Our song of love, like swollen oranges,
Delights my heart again with all your sweetness,
It lets me touch your face, your pool-black eyes,
Where is your liquid voice, where does it sing now?

How did you come here, Bernard? I ask him. How did you get away? But he won't say. He doesn't want to remember the long journey from the war in Mozambique to Skyline. Because when he remembers it, he must also remember war following him, stalking him, hiding behind the traffic lights, just over his shoulder.

All he says is that we must never think that war is like a hyena or a jackal or like locusts covering your fields. War is not an animal and it is not insects. War is the madness of people and nothing else. Once it has circled your home, your village, your family and shot up everything which makes up your life, war will hang out at the edges of your mind, waiting for you to walk out alone into the night. And then it lashes out at you with long terrible fingers to pull at your flesh and remind you that you should not have lived. You too should have been blown apart, burnt with all the others. War is not happy for anyone to survive. War is a mass grave. Those who escape the bullets walk away with a torn heart and eternal horror. This is what Bernard tells me. On the roof of Skyline.

Here, three paintings have been joined together to form one work titled *It is Time for the War*, though each is a distinctive piece. They have been hammered onto a wooden packing crate and should be studied from left to right before being viewed as a whole.

In the first we see again a modelling on Marc Chagall's work, this time his monumental *War*. It shows a column of fleeing people, some huddled in groups comforting each other, others weeping.

Ash-greys, blue-greys and grey-whites are relieved only by the strelitzia-orange flames in the background.

In the foreground a body lies spread-eagled on the ground.

A black bird with a yellow beak flies off into the distance.

At the right of the canvas we see two crucified children.

In the centre, at the top of the canvas, a weeping madonna floats in the air. From her arms falls the figure of a third child, plummeting to earth.

The second painting, placed in the centre, is based on Francisco Goya's *The Third of May 1808*. Here the artist has focused entirely on Goya's victim who is about to be shot at point-blank range by firing squad. Shrewd brush strokes capture his Omo-white shirt, his terrified eyes, his arms outstretched and evocative of a crucifixion. We are spared a vision of the firing squad and see only the ends of bayoneted rifles, fused together and entering the canvas on the right, unrealistically close to the victim's breast, and emphasizing the impossibility of escape.

The background is an unremitting black. On the left side of the victim lie the two pieces of a broken, despairing-grey calabash.

The third painting, on the right, is based on Pablo Picasso's *Guernica*. The artist has succeeded in portraying an apocalypse by using black, grey and white, with the odd touch of carmine, and with sparks of yellow thrown across the canvas.

It is a work which should have stood on its own, and it should have been executed on a much larger canvas. But the overwhelming despair it transmits, together with the pain and sense of useless slaughter, suggest that the artist would have been overcome by the horror and palpitation of the episode he was capturing, had he dared to express himself as hugely as did Picasso.

Chapter 18

Our mother hasn't gone to work for a few days. She's been sitting at the kitchen table smoking and drinking coffee spiked with brandy. She doesn't talk to anyone. She's been crying. I go to school and come back home and she's still sitting there. She says she can't make it without him. I'm not saying his name, okay? I told you already, his name is a dead word. But after a few days of her just sitting there, I ask where he is. She says he's got a flat in Wynberg and he's doing fine all by himself now that he's left her with me and Mossie. Lucky him.

I tell Raphael I'm going to fetch him. Not for me, you understand that? I never want to see him again. And I've told Mossie she never wants to see him again either. But our mother's been sitting around too long. I mean, if she was dead it would be one thing. Me and Mossie would just get on as usual. But she's just sitting there, hopelessly.

I leave Mossie with the Spice Girls and catch the train with Raphael. When we get to Wynberg station I tell him to go back: Don't wait. He'll drive me home. We're going home together. You go back on the train and I'll see you tonight.

So Raphael goes back by train and I see the difference between us. He can't ever go to fetch his dead father because his father is at the bottom of a lake wearing a suit and tie with muddy barbels swimming by. But me, I can fetch this man with the dead name. I can fetch him and he'll come back with me because our mother is losing her mind and he has to come home now.

His flat is tidy and dark and smells of him: cigarette smoke and CK cologne. His smell has gone from our flat now. Here the windows are all closed and the curtains drawn.

He's all strange and different. I feel stupid standing here. Must I hug him? Shake his hand? Must I say: Hey, don't you remember me and how I used to race down the stairs to fetch you? And Mossie? Have you forgotten Mossie, your Madelaine, your baby bird? Must I say I love him, I want him? Must I say his name? I don't know what to say. I tell him I've come to fetch him for our mother. I don't say his name. My voice sounds funny. I tell him that our mother is going crazy and he needs to come back. I don't know if I'm supposed to say something more and I hate myself for getting tied up inside.

No. He won't come back. He says he will never come back. He's left her now. *Understand?* He's left her and he can't come back. Ever.

He doesn't touch me and I don't touch him. I'm trying desperately to work out what happened. Something has disintegrated. I am not his daughter anymore. I am not anything to him anymore. And he is nothing to me. But why? What happened? Did I do something wrong to him? Did I fail him in some way? Is it Mossie? Mossie's problem? Has he grown ashamed of her? Me? All these questions crowd around in my mind.

He picks up his keys and I follow him out. I notice some oranges in a bowl on the kitchen counter and there's a loaf of bread, a packet of Joko tea and a half packet of chocolate digestives. I look at his back as I follow him, at his denim jacket and the shape of his hair. That's what I see on the way out of his flat in Wynberg and it becomes like a stain in my mind which I can never rub out.

He drives me back to Skyline and all the way there no one says anything. I look out the window on my side and he looks straight ahead as he drives. There's this pain inside me like a poem wanting to explode, but there is no wind, so the poem stays there burning and burning. And I know it will stay there forever, this pile of bad poetry aching inside me.

I have this longing, in his car, for the wind to blow and to batter against us, to throw us together and blow away everything that has gone wrong, blow it away like leaves. But there is no wind today. There is stillness and heat and moaning, disgusting traffic.

He drops me at Skyline, at the red robot. I want to say something but I can't. I want to say: Is this it? Are you just going to drop me here at the robot and not come in or anything?

But I say nothing. I get out of the car without even looking at him and watch him drive off as the robot turns green. I shout out: You shit! You piece of shit! But the traffic drowns my words. The traffic thuds onto my words like a beast of prey and devours them. There are no words in the air.

So this is something you need to know, now. I never cry for him, you hear? I never, never cry for him, not now or ever. But the burning sits there in the middle of me, like still wind. And only later, much, much later, when I am grown up and can think about it all, do I get a sense of the sorrow which was stuck in his throat. Only then do I understand why he couldn't look at me.

The next day our mother gets up and goes to work. After that she never talks about him again.

The eighteenth, large, panoramic painting shows a white man who has just arrived in Africa. He and his Land Rover Discovery are being rowed on a raft across a river by naked, black men.

The river is silver-green and the complementary silver eyes of crocodiles glint in the water.

This man, dressed in a khaki-coloured safari suit, puffs at a cigarette and reminds the viewer of the turn-of-the-century gentlemen-explorers who travelled down

Africa and then up again, collecting specimens of flora and fauna to be pressed and mounted for European museum collections.

From the deep and menacing foliage of the background, black faces with yellow eyes look out at him. A chameleon walks across the front of the canvas.

In the right-hand corner is a black-and-white photograph, slightly curled at the edges. It shows a woman standing at the kitchen sink looking out a window.

To capture the deepening of evening, the artist has used maroons and indigo-greens with sparse touches of majanji-yellow and gold.

The painting is titled *It is the White Man Crossing the River.*

Chapter 19

It's cats again, screaming in the night. But it's not cats. It's police cars outside with their blue lights flashing. Me and Mossie lean over the veranda and see a crowd of police and soldiers down below. The whole of Skyline has been cordoned off. They come up the stairs with dogs and search each flat looking for drug dealers.

They bang on our door.

Police! Open up! Open up!

Our mother opens.

Sorry ma'am, just a routine check.

They walk in, look around, check out Mossie, look at me. But they don't search us, they just take down our mother's name and write something on their clipboard. They leave us alone because she's a straight, white lady with two kids. They tell our mother she should think about moving from this block because it's become a bad place, full of dealers and illegal immigrants. She lights up another smoke.

The police polish up the whole of Skyline, up and down, every floor. They search the Nigerian who lives alone for over an hour and go through some flats twice but find nothing.

They tip up the Spice Girls' flat, pull the purple drapes from the windows, turn over the white couch, strip the beds, pull everything out of the cupboards, throw the beautiful wigs on the floor. When Alice protests they call her a moffie and tell her to mind herself or they'll throw her in jail anyway. They don't need a bit of dope to turn anyone in. They tell her she'll be thrown in with real men and raped to death, so she better shut her mouth when they tear open her bag and tip out her lipsticks and creams.

Mossie and I hang out on the veranda all night. She nearly falls asleep standing there, so I bring her back to bed and cover her. Then I sit alone and watch the blue lights flashing and watch all the people outside because it seems the whole world has come to see what's going on.

When the soft, pink light of the morning touches the sea down at the end of Long Street, I go to bed. I don't hear our mother get up or go to work.

Mossie climbs into my bed and we sleep right through the morning. She doesn't go to New Horizons and I skip school.

We make French toast, then go up to the roof and spit off the edge a while. We go back down the stairs to stretch time. We stop on the first floor and look in at flat 101, not sure why the door is wide open because Gracie and Cliff have gone to work. Because they work for the police, their flat wasn't searched either.

Everything is neat and in its place as usual. Except the Nigerian is sitting on their sofa with a little notebook. He is not their friend. I don't know how he got into their flat. Mossie and me go in and he smiles his big, white smile at us. All around the edge of the room are small packets, neatly stacked, flat against the walls. This is where the drugs were hidden, all night.

How did he know Gracie and Cliff never tap their canes inside the flat and never walk against the walls? He smiles us his big smile again as some guys from the fifth floor come in quietly, without talking. He ticks off in his notebook and they take what's theirs.

When Gracie and Cliff come home at six we go down and talk about the raid. Cliff tells us there must have been a tip-off because Skyline is the hottest trading post in town. That's why it's called Cocaine Court.

They got some inside information, that's for sure. We all know that. But how to pin them down? How to catch them? They're so polished, so slick.

He smacks his fist into the palm of his other hand and stares ahead with his milk-white eyes: *Man! It's all a sick joke. And where did they hide it? That's the question.*

We watch him make supper. He won't let us do anything: *No, I don't need help, thank you. No, as you see, I am the master of my own kitchen. Captain of my own ship. That's right. All you have to do is enjoy my food!*

He chops chicken into fine slithers and guides them into a pan of smoking olive oil. Then he adds spices, garlic and coriander, touching everything gently to see. He knows the distances between hotplates and kitchen counters and is guided by the heat from the stove so nothing spills or drops. There's rice steaming on the back plate and Indian breads in the oven. He wipes his hands on his apron, then through his hair, tilting his head to face the ceiling. He stretches out to the fridge and pulls out a beer: *You want a beer? Anyone want a beer? Gracie, what you drinking, sweetheart? What? Nothing? Are you feeling okay, Gracie?*

Gracie thinks the flat has a strange smell. She is sitting on the couch eating nachos with her legs crossed and up on the coffee table. Yes, she might as well have a beer. I open the can and bring it through to her. She looks pretty, the bowl of nachos in her lap, her big, brown, fake eyes looking across at nothing.

We carry the food from the kitchen and sit around the table. Cliff likes the setting to be perfect, so everyone has a serviette, the right cutlery and matching plates. He blesses the food: *Thank you, dear Lord, for what we have before us.*

We say *Amen* together.

Gracie switches on Frank Sinatra and Cliff dishes up the best curry I've ever tasted. *Good? Yes? You see what you can do with fresh coriander? Nothing like it. Nothing like it. Guess where I got the recipe? You got it!* Your Family, alright! *What does Mossie want? Tomato sauce? On my curry! Now I've heard everything!*

It's getting late. Gracie asks us to take Molly and Beth out for a last walk. We take them out with ordinary leads, not harnesses. Without harnesses they're not so serious and roll around on the ground.

We hang out a bit. Music is pouring out of the Whistle Stop Café. 7Eleven is bright and full. On the pavement, round the side where it's dark, I see a black girl. I watch her lay out cardboard, then wrap her baby up in a thin blanket and put him down without a pillow. Where have they come from and where are they going? The night will be kind. There is no wind and there is no rain. They will wake up before the sun and be gone by morning.

The traffic makes smooth sounds and smooth lights. The traffic is the madonna of the city. It wraps around babies and homeless children and holds them tight. It sees them sleeping in doorways and on pavements and caresses their hair with a gentleness. It hurries over them and then back again, stroking them through the night.

Me and Mossie take the dogs in, eat some of Cliff's apple crumble, then go up to the roof to find the moon. Mossie is dropping on her feet, so I take her in.

I lie awake for a long time. There is no sound from our mother. It's strange that I never see her buy brandy. I never see her finish a bottle or open a new one. It always seems as if the bottle is half full and it looks like she only drinks one glass. She keeps all her pills in her bag, never leaves any at home.

Next morning Princess finds Alice beaten and crumpled on the landing outside her flat. Her wig has been shredded, her satin high heels thrown down the stairwell. Her face is so beaten and her eyes so swollen that it is hard to see who she is. Only her perfume speaks of her grace and loveliness. Princess hoists Alice up in her huge, black arms and carries her into the flat, puts the white couch back on its feet and lies on it, holding Alice to her breasts, stroking her and soothing her with her molten voice. Alice is so broken that she cannot even cry. She just lies in the warm, fat, black arms Princess wraps around her, moaning through swollen, bleeding lips that Bluebell must be fetched from wherever she was thrown.

This painting, called *It is the Dealing on Long Street,* is of a drug dealer leaning against a corner wall under the blue sign of the Standard Bank.

He wears black shades and a black shirt with the sleeves cut off. His trousers are tucked into military boots.

The pavement on which he stands is strewn with Coke cans and bits of paper which show that the wind is blowing.

His slightly hunched shoulders suggest it is cold.

The colours are strong and evocative: greens, dry-river-browns and reds worked together without shadows.

The frame is made of orange Rizla packets stuck side by side onto card.

Chapter 20

If you look up Long Street at Skyline you realize what an ugly building it is, straight up and down with windows and verandas, blocking the view of the mountain. All the verandas have empty, cast-cement plant boxes welded to the rails, but only one veranda has any plants. It belongs to Mrs Clara Rowinsky, who is the only completely out-of-place person in this block.

In the first place, she has lots of money and is genteel and old and very old-fashioned. In the second place, she moved from a big house in Oranjezicht to live here in Skyline. She wears elegant things and has her hair done once a week. She lives in Skyline because it's just across the road from the Christian Science church and she is a serious member. She doesn't drive a car anymore so needs to live close by.

Mrs Rowinsky's flat is full of books and beautiful things: Persian carpets; carved wooden chests filled with embroidered white linen; a collection of blue and white porcelain; urns which she fills with wilted flowers and sprinkles with spices and fragrant oils. She is an art dealer and has a small gallery in Church Street. Here, in her flat, every wall is hung with oil paintings and framed water-colours. We often help her carry new work in because she likes to live with changing art.

One day, when we were helping her pack Christmas parcels for the Nazareth House AIDS babies she told us about her life. The parcels reminded her of other parcels and other times, when she was a schoolgirl in Berlin during the war, packing small things for people in hiding.

Her mother had died when she was little and she lived with her father and their housekeeper. Her father was a professor of linguistics at the university. The Jewish lecturers had been told to report for a roll-call, a registration. The meeting was just a Nazi set-up and those who went were arrested and sent off to extermination camps. Those who did not turn up were brutally beaten. Some were thrown over balconies, others killed.

Her father had a Jewish colleague who escaped this and disappeared into the underground. One night this colleague came to their house. Her father hurried him into his study and closed the door. They had a short and whispered meeting about which her father never spoke. But from then on he hid Jews from the Nazis, keeping up his job and pretences at the university.

When she was thirteen she began helping him. Not with much, she thought. Walking home from school, waiting on a certain corner for just so many minutes, then walking on home. She would be signalling, with that short wait, to an unknown person in the crowd to follow her. And that unknown person, time and again, sometimes a woman, sometimes a man, sometimes a grandparent, would tap on a window late at night and she would let them in to her father's study. Here they would stay until a signal arrived from somewhere that they should move on to a certain meeting point. From there they would be shepherded across a border, or around a roadblock to a new hiding place outside the city, or into a wood and into, perhaps, a few more days of freedom.

This haunting painting, titled *The Sorrow is Sitting on the Bench,* uses a silverish mixing of greens and blues with touches of yellow and red ochre to express a feeling of rain in the colour of the air.

We see three people standing at the side of the road in front of a bench at a bus shelter. Each wears an overcoat and boots. The two on each side are Nazi soldiers.

In the middle stands a girl with a yellow star pinned to her lapel.

On the bench sits a black bird with a yellow beak. The bus shelter carries a red advertisement incongruous for its time: *Always Coca-Cola.*

We focus on the faces of the three and see bewilderment in the rosy-cheeked face of the child and a cold sense of duty in the faces of the soldiers whose cheeks are also touched with the blush of youth.

The picture is not framed.

Chapter 21

It's Sunday morning and music is pulsing out of Skyline: marimba, rap, rave, Yvonne Chaka Chaka and plain old SABC. People wearing vests and shorts, wrap-around sarongs and sandals are washing cars downstairs, hanging out washing on verandas upstairs.

Raphael and me and Mossie cross over to the Christian Science church and sit at the back. Raphael wants to sketch the dome.

Mrs Rowinsky is up there in front. The organ music doesn't have a great beat. The Lutheran church bells clang away so we hear them in here and the traffic is still roaring. It's a Sunday roar, a worshipping roar, not a going-to-work-in-the-city roar. There are only about twenty people at the service counting us and Mrs Rowinsky. They're all old and sitting alone and mostly they are women so I suppose either their husbands are not into Christian Science or they're dead. Mrs Rowinsky runs the service with two other people: a thin, worried man and a dreamy lady who sings the solo hymns.

The thin man reads from the Bible and Mrs Rowinsky explains each portion. This all comes over on loudspeakers but you still have to listen hard because of the traffic. What she's saying is that mind is powerful and that you can change things for the good if you harness mind power.

This is what Mrs Rowinsky is into. She believes you can heal and change situations with your mind. I don't really believe that. If you think about it, even though she's lovely and kind, Mrs Rowinsky's thoughts haven't changed anything in Skyline. You still see lots of litter outside and street children and sad girls who just hang in, leaning against the building. No one ever bothers about them. I don't. And I don't pick up litter. There's no use, it all just blows in again.

The thing about the world today is that all people want is entertainment. There seems to be no wish for mind or anything with depth. Well, mind is everything. Everything. Mind will impart purity. Mind heals.

The Christian Science building is a bit plain for me but Raphael likes its clean lines. His sketch is beautiful.

I don't stay long. As soon as the next hymn starts I slip out with Mossie and hope Mrs Rowinsky hasn't seen me go because she likes to think I'm interested in all this. We sit on the steps outside watching the cars, waiting for Raphael. It's nearly eleven and he'll soon come out. I look up at Skyline and see, on one of the top-floor verandas, a fierce argument going on.

A man, dressed only in his underpants, and a woman in a pink gown are screaming at each other. Their words get lost in the noise of the traffic and are transported away as violent passengers. She turns fiercely to go inside and comes out with a pile of linen, then goes in again and comes out dragging a mattress. She throws sheets and pillows over the edge of the veranda and they fall the eight stories without screaming. Then she throws over the mattress and it lands with a thud down below without killing anyone. She goes in again and comes out with a pile of clothes and throws them out, one by one. They fall gracefully, like suicidal men, one after the other: trousers, shirts, a jacket, underpants.

The man leans against the veranda rail, sobbing. I watch him, his head hanging between his arms, his back heaving up and down. She is shouting and waving her arms around, her pink gown flapping in the confusion. Suddenly she stops and folds her arms. Then she goes up to him and puts her arms around his crying body. He straightens up, holds his face in his hands, leans towards her and buries his head between her breasts. They both go back inside.

Mossie is sitting with her head hanging between her knees. She knows something bad has happened to Alice and Bluebell and she is angry because no one will tell her what. She straightens up suddenly and glares at me, then sets off across the road and up the lift to the Spice Girls' locked door. She thumps on it with her two fists because she knows they are in there. I follow her up slowly, dragging my feet. We told Mossie they had gone away – they won a holiday to Durban – there was no time to say bye – they went to find beads for her – they kissed her goodbye while she was asleep. She knows this is all lies.

I don't stop her knocking and wait with her until Alice opens the door. I wait while she rams herself into Alice's bruised body and holds her tight. She does not look at the swollen face, at Alice's bandaged head without its glorious covering of curls, at the bruised eyes, the cut lip. She sees only that Alice's spirit has been broken and that Bluebell wants to die.

Mossie relates to all illness as she does to wounded birds: with quietness and calm and an understanding that if you flap around with a broken wing, the wing will not heal. She comforts the Spice Girls just by being with them, playing poker, making toast, chilling Cokes. She brings in a basket of beads and drapes strands around their necks while they sit stiffly propped up on the white couch. They have to recover. They have to get their wigs on again and paint up their faces. Mossie gives them lots of time for this but no choice.

In this painting, *It is the Park on Sunday,* oak trees are heavily adorned with green leaves. Flowers bloom in a frenzied splash of magenta and marigold-orange.

In the bottom corner lies the body of a woman dressed in a ball-gown. Her plum-coloured shoes float off into the air.

A middle-aged couple sit on a park bench eating fish and chips. They each look out of the canvas, the woman to the left, the man to the right, unaware of the wounded woman lying before them.

A black bird with a yellow beak flies behind them.

A vagrant staggers through the middle distance, his newspaper-wrapped gin bottle tucked into his pocket, his bleary eyes looking out of the canvas.

Chapter 22

Clara Rowinsky and her father were betrayed by their housekeeper. She had worked for Clara's father for twenty years and brought up his only daughter. She knew about the coming and going of Jews in the night.

The night the soldiers stormed her home and arrested her father, Clara Rowinsky was out, guiding a group of people through the darknesses of the city to a meeting point. They beat her father about the head and across his back and pushed him so he stumbled and fell at his doorway. A soldier kicked him. Another booted him in his back. They laughed as he grovelled on the ground for his glasses.

When she returned home she saw the doors flung open and the house ablaze with lights. Her father was gone. She slipped back into the shadows where the hidden people lived, those hiding and moving like shades. This is where she spent the rest of the war, with the underground resistance in the creases and folded places of the city. She was fourteen years old. She never found her father again. What she found were the tatterings and shreds of human dignity which murmur about in hidden places. She found torn, tortured, betrayed, burnt and broken people. She found fleeing, fearful people, and those with festering wounds.

The thing about betrayal is this. The betrayer is generally someone who knows you. Our housekeeper was a wonderful, motherly woman. Well, she was my mother, really. And I loved her. I can still conjure up in my mind the comforting, homely smell of her – flour, butter, steaming potatoes.

What made her turn? I don't know. The Nazi propaganda poisoned the sweetest souls. She was not educated, just a simple, country woman. Perhaps that was the root.

No, I don't hate her. I searched for her after the war, as I searched for knowledge of my father's fate. But everything was upside down then. The world was still mad and it was impossible to trace either of them.

I even searched the synagogues and the ruined Jewish homes, believing my father had escaped and been hidden by those he once helped. I searched Catholic churches – we were Catholic, you see – hoping that is where he had found shelter.

Yes, I was just a child then, but no longer a child. I had lost everything and innocence, belief in good. You see, you can't really go through those horrors and come out the same person. War is a terrible thing. The turning of human upon human is something I have never come to terms with. Yet life, true life, is something wonderful. We must hold this before us all the time. And we must work constantly at never being swallowed by the mindset of evil. Evil is always about and we must be aware of it.

Raphael and Mossie and me are with her in her flat. She is sitting in a deep armchair with her feet propped up on a leather stool. We've just eaten vegetable soup and whole-wheat rolls. I notice that her hands are as wrinkled as her face, that her joints are thick and the skin stained with brown age spots.

She has started running art classes every Saturday afternoon at the Pan African Market. Bernard has joined the group.

In the twenty-second work the artist uses chiaroscuro to suggest three-dimensional form with varying tones of light and dark paint.

A young woman sits inside a bomb-damaged cathedral.

Subdued ochres capture the closing light of early evening which seems to glow in the recesses of the building.

The viewer imagines the voices of angels lingering above the destroyed roof. Within the dark and light tones can be felt the sorrow of one waiting for the return of a loved one.

The artist conveys an expectation of movement to suggest that the young woman will open the great, carved, wooden door, supported on both sides by bullet-holed walls. We sense that she will walk through it into the world, all alone within twisting brush strokes and sinuous ribbons of greys, blues and gun-metal-silvers.

Chapter 23

Many years after the war I met the owner of the old Grand Hotel, Mr Bushinsky. He had survived the Warsaw ghetto uprising and he told me that he knew of my father, that my father had been in Warsaw and that he had survived the war.

Somehow he must have made his way from Berlin to Warsaw. It's impossible to know how. Or why. Warsaw was not a place to seek refuge in. Well, this was devastating news, news I dared not believe.

Yes, I wanted him to have survived but by the time I heard this news he would have been dead already, naturally, it was so many years after the war. I pursued this possibility, that he had escaped Berlin, survived, but then I had to let it go.

But what this stimulated in me was the whole question of shelter: the sheltering of the fugitive, the sheltering of the refugee from whatever circumstance but particularly from war and destabilization. My father had sheltered Jews and later I was sheltered by Russian soldiers and later still by nuns. And when I met my late husband I suppose he too sheltered me. Then coming here, to this new country, as a young bride, that was shelter, for I was still a fugitive, really.

The fugitive from war is a broken person, and you imagine that person arrives with nothing except what he can carry on his back or what he wears. But there is also what is inside him. What is inside of him is the realization, conscious or not, of the barbarism which hovers at the edges of our reality, all the time.

We are wrapping parcels again in Mrs Rowinsky's flat. Easter parcels this time, and we've just eaten nut roast and vegetables. Mossie has fallen asleep on the couch from eating too much. Raphael is sealing the boxes and I'm doing the ribbons. Inside each box we've packed a chocolate egg, a box of Smarties and a small bunny. Mrs Rowinsky is doing the labels.

Something else I have given a lot of thought to is the whole question of returning. How do displaced persons return home? What did the Jews of Berlin who survived come back to? What happened to my father's colleagues, those who might have survived? Do you think they just came back, back to their positions at the university, back to their homes? No. That was not possible. Our house in Berlin was not ours after the war. I went there, just to have a look and was turned away by a German woman who said it was hers and had been her mother's and before that her grandmother's and she closed the door in my face.

But I had seen our piano through the door. I knew that my father's office still housed all his books. But I could not return. No one returns after war. You cannot return to what you knew because everything and everyone is changed either by death or the pretence of forgetting what happened. No one remembers committing any atrocity. No one remembers stealing. No one remembers genocides or ethnicides. Isn't that extraordinary? But this is what war is about – murder and forgetting.

Sometimes in the deep night Mrs Rowinsky wakes up to a loud knocking at her door. She sits up, holding her breath, listening for the voices which have come to fetch her. She is a collaborator. She is to be branded with a number. She is to be gassed with the Jews. But there is no one at the door. She puts her head against the pillow and does not move until sleep envelops her.

When we finish packing, we wake Mossie up and carry the parcels downstairs, then wait for a Marine taxi to take Mrs Rowinsky up to Nazareth House. She doesn't like Rikkis.

Thank you, dears. I won't be away long. Come up later for hot chocolate if you're not busy.

We walk down to Waterkant Street and sit on the pavement. Raphael sketches the building opposite us: little balconies; plaster flowers; delicate edges; curls around windows. Then we walk around looking for old brickwork and make our way to Princess's hair salon in the Pan African Market.

Mossie brought a letter home on Friday saying she's got bird lice in her hair. I haven't done anything about it. But now I see her scratching so we take her up to Princess for a good wash.

Princess rubs a fine paste through Mossie's hair, wraps her head in a hot towel and tells us to hang around for an hour. We wander through the building, in and out all the rooms, looking at all the beautiful things for sale: bronzes from Benin; carved doors from Zanzibar; Ethiopian crosses; masks from Cameroon; cloth from Mali. Tailors sew up bright robes on old

Singer sewing machines and these hang with cotton pantaloons and loose shirts against the walls.

We go up to the first floor and sit in the food bar. Township jazz is twanging out of a ghetto blaster. Tie-dye cloths hang against the walls.

A woman brings us Cokes on a red, tin tray. One of her hands has been chopped off and her wrist is crudely rounded. She puts the tray down and scrapes our money off the table into the palm of her good hand. Her hand was cut off by rebels and thrown into the bushes, leaving a trail of red blood. Her hand was held down on a tree stump by boy-soldiers and chopped off with a machete.

The fine, bleached-white bones of her hand lie outside her door in Freetown up in Sierra Leone. One day she's going to fetch them back. One day she's going to look for those boy-soldiers to ask them why they did this terrible thing. And she will find many other bones of hands and arms and feet and legs piled up in the hot sun. And the boy-soldiers, now grown to men, will tell her the rebels stole them from their mothers and drugged them and beat them and forced them to do these things. And she will see that their eyes are not the eyes of wise men but the eyes of children trapped in killing fields. She will see in them the eyes of children forced to war. And she will be unable to be angry with them. She will understand these boys who have grown to be men in such a swift and terrible way.

So she will just gather up the bleached-white bones of her fingers, though they have no use, and leave these boy-men drinking in the bars where she found them.

Mossie's hair is finished. It's shining and smells of wood ash. We wait for Princess to lock her salon, then wind our way down the stairs, out into the traffic and back home up Long Street.

I hope bird lice haven't dropped off her onto Mrs Rowinsky's sofa.

This is the only head-and-shoulders portrait in the collection.

In it we recognize Evelyn de Morgan's study of the head of Jane Morris in old age for the painting *The Hour Glass*.

The white-haired woman tilts her head slightly to one side and her eyes, looking down, show her to be deep in thought.

She wears a yellow jacket. Tranquil overtones of olive green are drawn down from the background to a desert-melon-green surrounding her. These colours highlight the lead-white pearls around her neck.

On her right hangs a rosary.

Behind her, to the left, goose-step three Nazi soldiers, their heads turned to look out from the canvas at the viewer.

The painting has a wooden frame and is untitled.

Chapter 24

It's Monday. Raphael has to go home early to do something with his mother. We help Mossie balance on the rail while we wait for a Rikki. It's hard for her and she keeps falling off. Bernard arrives back from the Chinese Warehouse with new flags. I lean up against Raphael and kiss him on his mouth. He holds me close to him with his hands holding me just here. My whole body sparkles inside and I wish he didn't have to go.

Mossie and me help Bernard carry his flags upstairs. He's got some Cuban ones and Mexican ones.

I not thinking people like to buy these ones. What you think? The best ones for selling is the South African one. You know that? All the tourists they wanting Mr Mandela's flag. You wanting something to eat? We go down now to Italian shop?

Mossie and me race down the stairs and get down to the ground floor before Bernard reaches there in the lift. She holds one hand and I hold the other as we cross the road.

You cross carefully in this time. You see these cars be angry in this time. Five o'clock, they like those tsetse flies. Oh yes, like tsetse flies seeking out to bite us. Where your young man go so early, hey? He so nice fellow. Yes, surely, he be the fine young man, that Raphael.

The Italian shop smells nice and Giovanni is full of spirit. He has carefully combed, black hair and a thin moustache. He speaks Italian to Bernard and Bernard chats back in Portuguese.

Cappuccino per tre. Si! Si!

Bernard tilts his hat, feels whether his tie is right, glances at himself in the mirror behind Giovanni. His cup trembles as he lifts it.

Pasta. Basilico. Olio d'oliva he says to Mossie and she grins.

Everything in here is delicious. We stare through the glass at the cheeses, meats and pasta dishes. Bernard buys us a roll with mozzarella and tomato and we stand outside watching Long Street traffic. Bernard looks into it.

It is just so many tsetse, he says. And we laugh.

Mossie wants to buy yellow beads but I say no, not now, tomorrow. She waves her arms up and down hard and screws her eyes up. She wants me to know she's sick of always doing what I want, always tagging around me. Why can't we do what she wants, for a change? I don't feel like a whole debate about who really does the hanging around here, so I just tell her that's the way it is. Too bad, but she just has to do as I say. She kicks the ground.

Why that Mr Giovanni beat his wife? She so beautiful like white water. She so sad, like water with not the fishes. You see this the trouble, she marry someone angry like Mr Giovanni. You see she be too young, she too beautiful to marry with him. He like to keep her only in the shop and upstairs in the small room. I see her cry sometimes. You know her name? Morgana. She tell me one time when he not looking. That a beautiful name, Morgana. You think so?

We go back into the shop again and look at Giovanni close up. He is warm and friendly. His white apron is dusted with flour. His sleeves are rolled up above his elbows and his tight, white muscles squeeze out. He guides a large ham through the slicer and catches the thin sheets of meat onto wax paper, humming a snippet from Verdi.

Does he beat Morgana in the night, above the shop, when the shutters are closed? Does she cry quietly like a child bride, into her pillow so he can't hear?

Bernard says so.

She must look to one side only. Always to the other side if another man is coming. She must never look at the side where stands another man.

Bernard, you know these things?

Why surely, I know these things. He kill someone who look his wife. He make salami from someone who touch his wife!

Bernard! You're talking crap!

I never talking crap. You know me, I talking about what I know. You ever see me to eat salami from Mr Giovanni? I tell you not to eat it. And little sister Mossie, you also not to eat salami, you only to eating the cheese. Nobody is dead inside the mozzarella cheese!

Mossie throws back her head and laughs with her mouth wide open so you can see half-chewed roll and mozzarella.

Shut your mouth, Mossie, I tell her. You look disgusting. What do you want to show the whole world your insides for?

We all laugh while tsetse traffic rushes by. And just for a moment the war is gone from Bernard's brown eyes.

Mossie's prodding me on and on about the yellow beads. I shout at her. Okay! Okay! Man, sometimes you just want too much! Five minutes only, you hear? Five minutes for yellow beads, then home. Understand? She smiles. You know how Mossie smiles. So we end up staying with her till the shop closes, me and Bernard standing around like idiots waiting for her to find exactly the right kind of yellow beads.

We see the title of this painting on the window of the shop it portrays: *Mr Giovanni Shop in Long Street*.

It is highly coloured, heavily laden and worked in abrupt, short brush movements, resembling by its busyness, but not by its contents, a township shop.

The windows are filled with hanging hams, salami and cheeses.

In the background, on the right, is a portrait of Benito Mussolini.

On the left float a bottle of Chianti and a cup of coffee.

A sign on the door reads *Italian Panettone for Sale*.

The wooden frame is painted red, white and green.

Chapter 25

When our mother used to shout at him (I won't say his name), he just sat in his chair, drinking beer, like nothing was happening. She would shout and carry on so that my head nearly burst. Mostly she shouted about money but she also thought he had lovers in hotel rooms all round Africa. She said he picked up coloured girls and fucked them in those little rooms. She could tell. She could tell from how his clothes smelt when he came home and because on weekends he just rolled over in bed. Like he'd had a week of hard sex, and weekends he didn't need it.

Maybe he did fuck all week. I couldn't tell. Sometimes I thought about him loving our mother and I realized that could be pretty difficult. Because her body is hard. Her body never folds over to make a space for you. If you go near, her shoulder turns just enough to close you out. I can't remember when she last touched me.

She never has anything to do with Mossie. I care for Mossie. If I wasn't around, Mossie would be dead. She would drown in the bath or fall off the roof.

Sometimes our mother looks over at Mossie and her eyes linger over her a little bit. But that's about it. She goes to work, brings in groceries, lets us know her life is ruined because of us. That's all.

Once they had a big fight and she started hitting him. Well, not really a fight, because it was all one-sided. He wasn't responding, so she started to hit him, pounding on his chest with her fists and crying.

I got desperate. What does she want? What does she want? I thought he would hit her. He is a big man. He has big shoulders and big fists. He could knock her into the wall if he wanted to.

Don't! Don't! I tried to pull her away from him. Mossie was huddled up. Mossie's eyes were all screwed up and she had her fingers tight in her ears.

I can't remember how the fight stopped. I can't remember if he hit her or if she just fell over in a heap. Stop making me remember. I don't want to remember. You want me to find some nice things to say about them, don't you? Well, there's nothing nice to say. There's nothing for them inside me.

I used to love him. I can remember loving him. He was the first person I ever loved. I used to wait for him to come home every Friday night and run down the stairs when he rang the intercom.

He was a diver. He worked on oil rigs and for marine agents, so he travelled all over the country. He left every Monday morning and came back on Friday nights. Sometimes he was away longer than a week.

I'm not going to tell you what he looked like or felt like or about his smell or if he was gentle. And don't expect me to tell you what it was like the nights he wasn't home, and how it was wishing for him to be here. Those things belong to me. And anyway, I've made myself forget. These feelings are all dead, like his name.

The next morning, after the fight, she started screaming at me. I can't remember why. Maybe I swore at her because I was angry with her. Anyway, she screamed at me first. I started to cry. I don't cry easily, but I did that morning. So did Mossie. We walked down the stairs together and he sat down with us on the steps between the fifth and fourth floors. But his lift to Mossel Bay was waiting outside so he kissed us and left us sitting there.

You mustn't think I cry anymore. That was the last time I cried and it was a mistake. I cried by mistake, you see. I was younger then.

I didn't want to go to school that day but I also didn't want to stay in the flat. My eyes were all puffy and red and I looked awful. I forced Mossie onto her bus even though she was still crying and covered in snot. I went to school but stayed in the library the whole day because I didn't want to speak to anyone. When I came home I just sat on the veranda and told Mossie to leave me alone.

From my veranda I look down at the trees growing in the Lutheran church garden: purple jacaranda and palms loaded with bright, orange fruit.

From the roof I can see even deeper into the Lutheran garden and the minister's old house. It's a spooky house that's never been painted. I look at the roofs and office windows all around the city. I watch traffic and take its sound to sculpt words with. I use its roar and the way it flows and swirls around the foot of Skyline. Traffic reminds me not to think happy family thoughts.

Mossie's got bird lice again. Princess gives her another treatment.

As long you got the birds, you got the bird fleas, Miss Mossie. You don't think this the time now to leave the birds?

Mossie shakes her head.

In this picture, based on Walter Sickert's *La Hollandaise*, we see a naked woman reclining on a bed in a sparsely furnished and ill-lit room.

She has been painted with a cruel and exacting economy of colour and warmth.

Her face is not visible in the half-light of the room, but her naked body is exposed by brisk scrapings of protea-silver-greens and ash-whites.

Because of the poor light, she looks older than she is.

We see a man entering the room from the left side.

Above the bed hangs a crucifix with a naked, white woman nailed to it. Her head hangs limp against her shoulder and her long hair trails to the side as if the wind is blowing.

This picture is titled *She is Selling the Love in the Brown's Hotel.*

Chapter 26

It looks like it, but we're not waiting for Cameron and Liberty Chizano to arrive. It's a hot night and we're just sitting on the veranda waiting for some air to blow. We notice a truly battered pick-up go by about ten times, all the way round the block and back to Skyline. It pulls up down below.

Two large Africans and a very thin one are crammed into the front and the back is laden with stuff covered by a tarpaulin.

The pick-up parks, but no one gets out. After a long time waiting for a breeze Raphael says it's time for him to go. Me and Mossie go down with him to wait for a Rikki.

The three people, two men and a woman, are leaning against their car looking up at Skyline, from veranda to veranda, window to window. They seem to have come a long way because the vehicle is covered in dust and so are they. We don't say anything to them.

Next morning when I walk Mossie to the bus, the pick-up is still there. One of the three is leaning against it looking up and down at the verandas and windows of Skyline. There's no sign of the other two.

They have driven from Zimbabwe to nobody in particular, just to our address: *Skyline. Long Street. Cape Town.*

It takes a few days for them to connect with the

Zimbabwean wire-workers who live in flat 300 and to make an arrangement with them. They offload the pick-up and we watch them carry in masses of wooden and stone carvings. I wait with Mossie because she wants to watch.

Cameron Chizano is the one she singles out because he's got a string of beads around his neck. She follows him into the foyer and as he puts down his load to push the lift button, she reaches for his beads. He leans down to her and lets her finger each one. She has never seen beads like these before: clear, orange amber, black ebony and silver. She holds onto them as he tries to straighten up, but it's like the first day in the Bead Shop all over again.

I go close to her and say firmly: Mossie, you can't have his beads. Okay? Just let him go. Hear me? Other people are also allowed to do beads. Mossie, you listening to me? Of course she's not listening. I might as well go sing to the moon.

And then Cameron Chizano does something really, really cool. He says she can borrow them, takes them off and ties them around her neck. They're threaded on a leather thong and she stands quietly with her eyes closed as he ties it.

Did you hear him say borrow, Mossie? Not have. Borrow. But she's not listening to me and I know her eyes are glowing even though they're shut.

From then on Mossie visits him every evening. He

and Liberty hire half a room in the Zimbabwean wire-workers' flat. They've packed it tight with carvings they've brought here to sell: hippos, tortoises, giraffes, masks, boxes, walking sticks. They each have a roll-up mat and some blankets and nothing much else. Except beads. Lots of beads.

I tell Cameron maybe he shouldn't show Mossie his beads. But he doesn't realize there might be a problem up ahead and he lets her see his cloth bags of amber, ebony and silver. Mossie has found the god of beads.

She spreads a sleeping mat and pours out the beads from their little cloth bags. They don't look like gold or diamonds, they look better, more beautiful than any bead she has ever seen in her life.

She's kneeling on the ground looking at them, touching them, sorting them. She takes handfuls of amber beads and holds them against her face. They smell of something. What is it? Smoke? Dust? Heat? She doesn't know. She pours a pouch of carnelian beads out across the mat, then draws them together into a neat pile. She leans down to them, lays her face against them, closes her eyes and a warmness fills her body so she starts to cry.

Cameron kneels beside her and lifts her gently from her crouched position. He gathers up the carnelian beads and pours them back into the pouch and gives it to her. He tells her about the slaves these beads were to have bought and makes a picture for her of ancient

Portuguese trading vessels crossing between India, the land of agate beads, and Africa, the land of slaves. He describes the storms which splintered the trading ships and tore at their sails. He tells her about the waves which claimed all the beads down to the seabed.

Mossie can feel the tides moving with the moon and raking among the sands and shells of the sea floor. She can feel the tides gathering up the orange-gold beads and scattering them up onto the beach to glitter for her: hundreds of carnelian and agate jewels, chiselled by bead-workers and weathered on the seabed. She imagines herself crawling across the sands, gathering them up. Because she has no words, her heart is beating fiercely.

Liberty looks out across the city from the veranda. Tomorrow she and Cameron will look for a trading place in St George's Mall to sell their carvings. The wire-workers will introduce them to the merchant who controls the pavement space and who will charge them protection because they are kwere kwere, foreigners who are not really welcome here. Sometimes traders from Africa get beaten up because people think they're stealing jobs.

The third person who travelled with them has moved in with Ghanaians upstairs. Cameron and Liberty met him at the border post and gave him a lift to Cape Town. He walked from Ghana to Zimbabwe and is so thin that he is almost a hollow reed. His name is Kwaku.

This painting, *In the Harare Township,* is of a barefoot, black boy standing in the dirt road at the edge of a township. He is wearing an adult's very large jacket which is frayed at the hem.

He has thin legs and his tattered schoolboy shorts are too small.

Behind him is a line of shacks, slightly tilted with small windows.

It has been raining. The dirt road is covered in puddles.

The artist's brisk use of grey-blues and post-tempest-grey makes the viewer feel cold.

The frame is of twisted wire threaded with bottle tops.

Chapter 27

Liberty is a poet. She doesn't write her poems down, she just makes poetry in her spirit and sings it with a huge voice. She's huge herself. Not fat really, just big with strong arms and legs. Also, her poetry doesn't sit inside her like mine does, like hot wind wanting to explode. Hers just explodes through a voice you could hear across a valley.

Her poetry is about war. It's not Bernard's war in Mozambique. This is the Chimurenga war in Rhodesia. In her war she was a fighter, not a refugee. And she won her war. So she is not like Bernard. She is bold and full of courage and she does not have fevers like he does.

I don't understand the words she sings because they're all in Shona. But I can tell from how she moves and the deepness of her voice that this is war here in the wire-workers' flat. I won't ever bring Bernard to listen to her. It will be more fire and fever for him and he won't cope.

When she sings in her language, I can see the mountains she walked over and I feel the weight of her AK47. I hear children crying and people running, running, running from Ian Smith's army. I see her sitting around a small fire deep in the Chimanimani mountains with the other freedom fighters. I see the blackness beyond the light of the crackling fire and cannot tell what is in the darkness. I smell the smoke of the fire and the sharp smell of the ground and the trees and the night. I hear her throw her old name away and rise up to become Liberty. A combatant. A woman who fights for freedom.

She has long dreadlocks with beads threaded into them which Mossie nods about and lets her keep. When she pounds on the floor with her legs, waving her arms, waving her pretend AK47 and throwing her voice, she tosses her head back and forth and sideways so that her dreadlocks lash out into the air, into the wind, into the mountains where she fought.

When she performs her poetry, the wire-workers listen closely and nod and say: *Yes. Yes, this is how it was.* They drink beer and Cameron opens another bottle and it gurgles down his throat. Sometimes one of them gets up and dances alongside her, in a stamping war dance. But it's a memory-of-war dance. It's not a dance for getting all steamed up to go kill someone.

Actually, it's usually very sad. I've been there once when someone with a saxophone visited and he played alongside her even though he had never heard her poem before. But he played the same way her poem cried out its tale, and I could tell he had also fought the war in Zimbabwe. I could tell he had been in the mountains and fired across the valleys. And that he had carried dead comrades across the river and buried them under moonlight. All this I knew just from his saxophone and the way it wove around Liberty's voice.

This picture is of a black girl wearing a ragged dress. The dress is red with white spots and has a white Peter Pan collar. She has outgrown it and we notice her young breasts pushing tightly against the buttons. Her legs seem too long because the dress is short on the body of this adolescent girl. She is not wearing shoes.

She sits on the steps of Cashel Valley Trading Store and we see a Coca-Cola sign painted beneath the name of the store.

In the foreground a thin, mangy dog upturns a bin.

To the side blooms a tree in scarlet.

Trundling in from the right is a military vehicle. A soldier leans from the window, smoking.

Despite the vigorous, angry brushwork of dark outlines and bright, thickly painted colours, the picture conveys a certain tranquillity.

Chapter 28

One night when Senhor Filipe de Oliveira drove into town to visit the woman he loved, Senhora Sofia Isabel de Oliveira called Bernard into her bedroom. He was not allowed into the bedrooms late at night. He cleaned them during the day and early each evening drew the curtains, lit the lamps and pulled back the bedcovers.

She called him into her room and told him to take off his clothes. Bernard was afraid because if the Senhor came home, he would shoot him. But he could not disobey his Senhora because he was her servant. So he took off his white serving tunic, undid the buttons of his shirt and let it slide off his shoulders. He untied the cord of his white pants and let them slip off his hips to the ground. He slid his rubber sandals from his feet and stood in front of her on the red and richly patterned Persian carpet.

She lay on her bed, her hair untied and beautiful against her white skin. The lamp threw shadows across the ceiling. Her eyes caressed his muscular body which carried no extra flesh on it but was strong and hard from toil. His sweetly pungent body odour reminded her of the warm comfort of the black servants she had known since she was a child.

My Senhora, she lying there and she got on that white lace and she put her hand to call me, but I too afraid. Really, I too afraid. So I just standing there and she looking me without the clothes and she call me to touch her. So I touch her. She has the soft body, my Senhora, and her skin is like the white flowers, those flowers I see opening only in the night when the moon is shining. And after that night, every night that the Senhor he go to visit the woman he love in the town, my Senhora call me to her room. My Senhora call me and I take off all the clothes so she just looking at me. And sometimes I to touch her, only as she wishes. And always I afraid that the Senhor come back and he kill me. I know he shall peel my skin to kill me slowly because he find me like this as I touch the body of my Senhora.

I learn the first time then from my Senhora how it is the loneliness. This the loneliness as I know it now. I only to know the loneliness for the first time when my Senhora she show me because I see the sorrow in her eyes and the tears they sitting on her face and shining. I see the loneliness be like maybe the rain forget to come. And those grasses and those trees they waiting for nothing.

We are in Bernard's flat. He has bought custard cakes and we are sitting on his mat eating them. Mossie is messing around with his flags and he gives her a big South African one. She shows him that she wants to play dress-up, so he takes some of his clothes and ties down from their hangers. We all put on jackets and Raphael puts on a hat. Mossie ties a cravat around her hair and goes off to fetch strings of beads. Bernard tilts a red beret across his brow and lights a cigarette. Outside, traffic keeps going somewhere and coming back again.

This painting, *It is the Senhora and the Love for her House Boy,* is of a gentlewoman's bedroom in which a great moth flies towards a gas lamp.

The colours of its wings – mustard-browns and soft beige – compliment the transparency of the lamp glass. These colours seem to capture a soft and moaning loneliness.

The woman's curls lie against the silk bedding, black against cream-white.

At the foot of the bed stands a naked, black man. He stands poised and exquisitely sculpted as if from black marble. His skin shines in the lamplight.

Floating in the background are a white tunic, white pants and a white apron.

Chapter 29

Mossie brings a letter home from the New Horizons social worker saying she wants to do a home visit. This is because Mossie keeps coming to school with bird lice, without her school bag, has mood swings and is usually very tired. This is not good news. If the social worker sees how we live she'll take Mossie away. If she takes Mossie away, I'll never get her back.

We show the letter to Alice and Bluebell. They know it's not wise to get on the wrong side of social workers and that this letter spells trouble. Mossie looks pale and suddenly throws up all over the carpet.

Alice and Bluebell work out what has to be done. From now on Mossie has to go to them before school to have her hair brushed and her uniform checked. They buy her a spare school bag and we ask the bus driver to look out that her bag stays on her back. But we also have to set up the ideal home, so we wait for a weekend when Raphael's mother goes to Port Elizabeth to play in a bridge tournament.

Alice phones the social worker, introduces herself as our Aunt Alice and invites her to Saturday lunch at Raphael's house up in Oranjezicht.

The social worker arrives in a blue VW Beetle and bangs the knocker with great authority. Alice meets her at the door, shakes her hand and leads her into the sumptuous Red Room. This is a room carpeted with Chinese silk rugs, hung with two Irma Sterns and a Pierneef, and filled with antique furniture. Large bronze urns stand in the corners.

We are all thoughtfully placed. I sit in a deep armchair with a copy of *David Copperfield* at my side. Mossie sits in an armchair with a teddy and a doll. She has been scrubbed and dressed up in a pink dress and looks a bit pale. Our Aunt Alice sits on the red, leather sofa sipping mineral water, dressed in a steel-grey Jenny Button trouser suit with a single strand of pearls around her neck. Her hair is brushed back sleekly, her make-up is light and she has tiny pearl studs in her ears. She looks lovely and rich and smells of Coco Chanel.

The social worker sits primly on a Louis XIV armchair, sips a Martini and looks over her gold-rimmed glasses at Mossie, who is as stiff as a photograph, clutching the teddy under one arm and the mock-Edwardian, white, porcelain doll under the other.

Mossie deals out cards in her mind and concentrates on a game of poker. Her eyes stare ahead and her thoughts work forcefully: *Let the social worker show her cards first. She must open the game, put her cards on the table.* Aunt Alice graciously allows the social worker to list all the problems Mossie brings to school.

Mossie's eyes drop into a squint and she manoeuvres her thoughts: *Calculate each of your moves but let her move first. Let her chuck down one card after the other. Don't play your strong cards yet.* We listen to the social worker catalogue Mossie's bad influence at school. Aunt Alice says nothing.

Mossie opens her eyes wide and fixes her gaze on the chandelier: *Mind the joker. I see a joker. There is not supposed to be a joker in poker.* The social worker wants to motivate that Mossie be made a ward of the court and placed in an institution. She also wants her medicated to control mood swings. Alice sips her mineral water and the social worker joins her hands as if in prayer, stretches her fingers so they stand upright like blades.

Mossie's thoughts wade through a tense game: *Gather the four aces to flatten her kings. Don't react. Let her win one hand, two, then wipe her face with a trump.*

Alice is cool, keeps the discussion tight, speaks with authority and a deep, gentle voice. *Yes, indeed there has been some recent neglect, but not intentional. No, not intentional. There has been some marital stress, yes, but nothing serious. Yes, the child needs structure, without doubt, she shouldn't run amok, should get eight hours deep sleep, should be free of parasites. Yes, the parents have gone for help with their problems and yes, the girls already live here with me. So let's not rush into medication. I would rather we assess Madelaine's behaviour within this new structure. I'm sure structure and routine will be sufficient to settle her, don't you? Well, let's give it a try, shall we? She's nearly thirteen, after all, and I'm sure we'll see her maturing nicely.*

Alice tells the social worker that she will employ an

au pair to be with *Madelaine* every afternoon and that in future she, Alice, will liaise with the school authorities. *Yes* and *Yes* and *Yes. Now let's go through for lunch, Miss French, and don't worry about a thing. We'll work as a team, you and I.*

The social worker does not feel comfortable. She's not sure, but she thinks she is being conned. But she can't say so outright and she can't quite work out what's wrong with the set-up here.

Raphael has laid the table with an antique, embroidered tablecloth, his mother's favourite Royal Doulton dinner service, silver cutlery and crystal glasses. We sit down to dinner, me, Aunt Alice, the social worker and Mossie. Mossie sits stiffly at table, pecking at her food, still playing poker in her mind with freedom for stakes.

Raphael and Bluebell help his mother's cook, Prudence, in the kitchen. Bernard serves at table. He wears a white waiter's suit with a red cummerbund and red fez and brings the food around to each of us on silver platters. He looks solemn and keeps his eyes down as good servants should.

The dinner is magnificent. Prudence has prepared smoked salmon, French onion soup, lamb with roast potatoes and buttered vegetables followed by strawberry frappé for dessert. This is rounded off with Black Forest chocolate cake, Italian biscotti and coffee with a touch of liqueur which Bernard serves in the Red Room.

Mossie concentrates on the last hand of cards playing through her mind. Her thoughts shuffle and deal swiftly as Aunt Alice concludes the afternoon and the social worker finally goes home, not convinced but not hostile either, her stomach tight as a stuffed pig's.

Alice falls back onto the red leather sofa and kicks off her shoes. *Now that's one tight-arsed little miss. You should have seen her, Bluebs. Knickers tied in a serious knot there. And as for that little frock, I mean really, someone should tell her tight skirts are a definite no-no for her thighs. Some hefty meat there squeezed into that little corset. Pass me the whisky, Raphael.*

Bernard drinks a beer without stopping for breath. *You see how she eating the cake? You think she never see the chocolate cake before? Little sister Mossie, maybe you to take the chocolate cake every day, then she not make trouble for you. What you think?*

Mossie is too exhausted to think. She climbs into Alice's arms and closes her eyes. Raphael finishes the cake, Prudence makes herself some tea and Bluebell pours a double whisky. Then we start cleaning up. It takes a long time.

In this complex painting, *It is the Lunch Party for the Little Sister,* we see the influence of two masters.

Three angels sit at a table and we note the same graceful positioning and posture of Andrei Rublev's angels in his *Trinity*. They wear long translucent robes, and although the slight tilting in each head expresses serenity, we see strength in their bodies.

The table setting is fashioned on Auguste Renoir's *The Luncheon of the Boating Party*. Bottles of wine, bowls of fruit and a crumpled tablecloth speak of the end of a large meal.

The delicate brushed-gold of the background is disturbed by a small, winged VW Beetle flying in to upset the tranquillity of the picture as a whole.

Chapter 30

When we get back to Skyline, tired and stuffed with food, we see Kwaku sitting on the step outside. He looks grey and his face is sweating. He lifts a hand to stop us, to ask us to help him up. Mossie flaps her arms and starts running around in circles. I tell her to cool it. This is the wrong time for racketing.

Raphael leans down to him, takes a thin arm across his shoulder, then lifts him to his feet.

Kwaku is light as a bird. What's wrong? He's so thin, thinner than river reeds. We take him up to the Ghanaians' flat. His mat is near the kitchen. Raphael helps him to lie down and takes off his sandals. He is in so much pain that we send Mossie to quickly fetch Mrs Rowinsky, who calls her doctor.

Kwaku is dying, wasting away. He'll be dead in a week. Mrs Rowinsky's doctor checks him out: *I'm afraid there's nothing I can do. Only relieve his pain.*

Mrs Rowinsky gives us a quilt and a mattress. *We can only keep him comfortable, dears.*

She shows us how to drip water onto his lips and trickle it into his mouth because he must be thirsty. Mossie rocks back and forth on her knees next to Kwaku's mattress. She acts as if one of her birds is sick. She cheeps softly. I don't stop her. Mossie is very kind. This is her way.

Kwaku reaches out to Raphael, takes his hand in his

weak, bony fingers. He wants to go back home. He
wants to die in his mother's arms, not here, far away
from her.

He came to Cape Town when Mr Mandela became
president and opened the new South Africa. He came
here with just his small rucksack because he had
nothing else and he wanted to make a lot of money.
Now he wants to go back and for his mother to hold
him while he dies. He wants to take his bicycle and
that cardboard box he points to.

His mother runs the Hollywood Bar, up in Africa
somewhere. It is a small bar on the edge of the jungle.
She brews up beer and sells it while all around the
birds screech. Roasting on an open fire are the torsos
and limbs of gorillas and chimpanzees which she buys
from bush hunters. She serves them and the succulent
charred heads and hands with mtoki and Pearl's Chilli
Sauce.

Kwaku's mother wears a robe of coloured cotton
and her skin is like the dark night shone up as brass in
moonlight. She smells of foliage and lush flowers.

Kwaku hears her voice in the traffic. It is the song
of jungle birds and when he hears her sing to him,
his pain lifts. He lies still, without moving, under
Mrs Rowinsky's quilt. But he feels his mother rock
him, rock him, as the jungle leaves shimmer and drip
wonderful juices down onto his dry lips. He whispers
to her that he has a bicycle and that in his box are two

blankets, an umbrella, a cooking pot, a teapot and six tin mugs. He has brought these for her. From South Africa.

His friends in the flat sit quietly and wait. They don't move and they say nothing. So we say nothing. They wait with him all week and then on the Friday he hears his mother sigh above the traffic and feels her close his eyes for him and rock him in her arms.

Kwaku's friends sigh with a sad song and beat on a little drum and we know he has gone back home. They beat on the little drum all night to mark his way, so his spirit doesn't get lost and wander around forever in the streets of Cape Town. They tell us of Kwaku's ancestors stepping forward from the dark regions to thank the drummers for guiding him home and then stepping back into the darkness.

Mrs Rowinsky stands at the window and looks out over the roofs of Long Street which in her mind have become the roofs of Berlin. And down below in the street she watches Nazi soldiers herding Jews towards the station. She watches the column of people snake its way through the streets and she trembles inside.

She turns to face the room and watches Kwaku's friends cover him with a cotton cloth. But she is in Berlin again, watching the covering of an old woman and listening to the hurried prayers, seeing the family flee down the stairwell, silently weeping, then joining the throng for there is no escape.

Mossie pulls me up to the roof and points at flying birds with both hands, spreading out her fingers. She wants me to know that Kwaku has flown away.

This, the thirtieth image, is painted to resemble a black-and-white photograph.

A thin, black man, so thin his joints look like balls under his skin, and a white youth, strong and with curls falling onto his face, are entwined together.

The white youth holds one arm around the black man's back and the other across his shoulder.

In the background hangs a cotton kikoi. A bicycle is propped against it.

Two neatly folded blankets are heaped on the left side and an enamel pot sits on the right. In the foreground are a 10 kg packet of bread flour and one of white sugar.

Beneath the blankets, we read the title: *It is the Treasures Bought from Heaven*.

Chapter 31

There is club life all day and night down Long Street. We're not supposed to go into the pubs and clubs but everyone knows us, so we just stroll past the bouncers. We've watched strip shows and seen hookers call in their clients. We've watched the Sultan, wearing black sunglasses and tightly tailored suits, cruise with his boys to collect protection money. We know how he leans on new bars and pubs till they have to pay him or close.

He saunters into the Lounge Café and orders drinks for himself and the boys. Ceiling fans chop the air which is heavy with cigar smoke. When the drinks come he wipes the tray off the table with the flat of his hand so the glasses and bottles crash down, washing the floor with whisky and beer. The waitresses turn away, show only the sharp cut of their hair and their white shoulders in black crop-tops. Customers look intently into their drinks or across their tables into the thick air. Then he saunters out, the Sultan with his boys.

Next night he leans on the bar and does the same again. His gold and ruby rings flash. So you have to pay, if you want to keep open. Then you can sell crack and be as cool as you like, wearing a little, black bowler hat and red bow tie. There's no big deal about all this. I'm just telling you so you know.

The best place is not actually in Long Street. It's a shebeen on Bree Street run by Mama Luke. She is a fat, coloured lady who brews beer and fries vetkoek with mince. The shebeen is an old house that friends of Mrs Rowinsky once lived in. *Once that was a good part of town.*

You walk in and all that is left of the old days is the grand, wooden fireplace with blue tiles around the inside. The grate is broken, the floor is worn black. People sit on crates drinking brew and smoking. There's a bare bulb burning in the middle of the room.

In the side room the Ou Kaapse String Orchestra plays through the night: three violins, a double bass, a banjo, a guitar and six old men with worn-out leather faces and bony hands. They wear bomber jackets and can hold a smoke in their lips while they play.

We wait for Bernard to get his drink, then stand with him around the string orchestra. Everyone smells of sweat and smoke.

The music is flat with the same tempo, same rhythm, and you think you've heard it before but you're not sure where.

When the orchestra plays, people sway. Princess is sitting with Cliff and Gracie on crates in a corner. She smiles over at us and shouts something but her words pound out into the rhythms of the orchestra. Cliff is slapping the tempo on his knee and Gracie is drinking Hansa from the bottle.

They haven't always done clubs. When they first moved into Skyline they spent every evening alone in their flat and went to bed early. They went to church on Sundays and Braille Bingo drives every second Saturday. One Saturday when their Bingo lift couldn't fetch them and they were all dressed up with nowhere to go, Raphael said they should come with us to Mama Luke. They sat stiffly on crates until they got their social bearings right. Quite soon the smoke and the smell of sweat and booze percolated through their senses. They loosened up and poured back the drink. They stamped out rhythm and had better fun than winning Bingo. Now they do the clubs every night except Sunday.

They're not sure why, but the Nigerian always insists on seeing them safely around the town at night. So they don't have to bother with their guide dogs and they never get hassled by street thugs. We know he owes them, big time, but of course we say nothing.

When the musicians stop for a drink Raphael and I sit on the front step and talk about nothing special. I lean up on him and breathe in how he smells. The air is cold outside. The music starts up again and people sway some more. We listen to the bass player called Babe droning on about someone called Lola. I want to know who Lola is. Raphael thinks it's Babe's lover. But Babe's got no teeth. How can you have a lover when you've got no teeth? We laugh. I love how Raphael laughs.

Every night Mama Luke gives the leftover vetkoek to a group of street children. She says she can only feed five or six of them. She can't deal with the whole crowd of urchins in Cape Town – Mr Mandela must also pull his weight. She lets them sleep in the back room of the shebeen as long as they don't sniff glue.

Mossie's in with them now making up new cigarettes from stompies they've collected. She knows I'll hit her if she lights up with them.

Bernard buys them Cokes and we stay there the whole night. When it's time to go we find Mossie curled up with the other kids and Bernard carries her home. He puts her on the bed, takes her shoes off and pulls the covers over her. Her hair spills across the pillow. *She look an angel,* he says. Raphael makes coffee and we take it up to the roof to watch the sky wake up. We look down across Long Street and watch a drunk swagger and stumble. The muezzin calls.

I ask Bernard if our mother has ever spoken to him. He takes a long time to answer and I think he has not heard me ask or maybe he does not want to say anything. He stands very straight with his hands in his jacket pockets and looks down at his shiny shoes.

Yes. Always she say good morning or good night if she sees me when I am coming. One time when those security outside Kiss Kiss Bazaar stop me and push me down because they want to know where I stealing my parcels, your mother she coming past. And she say to the security, that one with the big chains on his neck, that she know me. So they to leave me alone. And one time she give me the cigarette in the lift. But that time she say nothing.

The edge of the world turns pink and the traffic is like a prayer.

This painting, called *It is the Mama Luke from Bree Shebeen*, is of a fat, coloured woman with rolled-up sleeves wearing a white apron.

She has big, ham-like arms and rolls under her chin.

Her head is covered with a white doek and she is sitting on the steps of a dilapidated Cape Dutch house, holding a bottle of Castle in one hand and a cigarette in the other.

Sitting with her on the steps are two barefoot, ragged street children.

The house is painted white and the background sky a strong and bright blue.

Castle bottle tops have been stuck around the canvas to form a frame.

Chapter 32

You always wanting to know how I am come to Skyline. I walking here from there. I walking from Mozambique. Even through that Kruger animal park and I coming with some others through the fence. I too afraid and some others they get lost. We too hungry and too thirsty. And one time when there is nothing to eat we catch the snake and we eating that meat. And even some others the lions find them and eats them.

Nobody help me. And I not speaking the English that time. I stop by many places in the small towns and I try to show the madams please to give some bread. Not even money. And the madams wherever I stop they cannot give anything. And I see this. If you not to looking nice then the madams thinking you stealing and they too afraid. So I know I must get the nice clothes.

I stop one day in the small town. My feet is bleeding and my heart too is bleeding. My heart is broken. Then I go to the garage where is working the Portuguese madam. She owning the garage and she got her house at the back yard. She understand I not there to be stealing and she give me the job.

I work for this Portuguese madam and sleep in the back room on the floor. She give me the bread and coffee every day and at the end of the work to digging the pit she pay me the ten rand and the calendar. I not to know this is little money. But she give me the old shirt and trousers and the shoes. So I start to look good. And then I find the truck is going to Cape Town and I hide inside.

I am leaning over the edge looking down into the lights of Long Street listening to Bernard. The traffic is thick already. I hang my arms down over the edge and let them go limp.

Bernard stood in front of the Portuguese lady at the garage, torn, ragged and coated with despair. He asked for help. He wanted to say to her that he had journeyed an impossible journey away from war and was seeking shelter. He wanted to show her his swollen feet, cracked and bleeding like the clay of a dry waterhole. He wanted to say, when he heard her Portuguese words and saw her black hair piled up upon her proud head, that he was from her country, from Mozambique, that he was the houseboy of his Senhora, that he was seeking water to wash his wounds.

He wanted to tell her that he had gathered up the fingers chopped from his Senhora's hands and wrapped them in his apron and buried them, hastily, hastily, so that they would not be trampled by army boots. He wanted to say that he had crept back to the house sometime in the middle of the nightmare to fetch her body, but that it had been nailed to the door of the tobacco shed and shot through and through and through so that there was only muck left of her. But he said nothing of this. He said nothing of the mutilated body of the Senhor which had been hacked to pieces and thrown to his own dogs. He asked only if she had a job for him. He did not ask if his wife had perhaps come this way, a tall woman wearing a faded, floral-print dress, carrying nothing. Perhaps also with bleeding feet. Perhaps with – no, that would have been impossible – perhaps with three children walking beside her.

The Portuguese garage owner said no. She had enough boys working for her and there were hundreds always looking for work. This was a small garage. What did he think, that she must employ every Mozambican who came by?

Next day she saw Bernard outside at the pick-up place hoping for a lift or a job or anything. She sent her petrol boy to fetch him. She said he could dig the pit out back and he could sleep in the storeroom.

He dug the whole day and she gave him coffee and bread when evening came. He can't remember eating that bread. Maybe he just swallowed it whole. He dug the hard ground for a week, blistering his hands, then wrapping them in plastic bags when they began to fester. At night he slept on spread-out newspapers and listened through his exhaustion to the woman screaming at her husband and to his hot and ugly voice beating back at her like a raging bull. After a week of digging she gave Bernard ten rand and a Total garage calendar.

She never looked at black people closely because she hated them and was afraid of them. But this boy –

there was something about him. So she also gave him a bundled-up pair of trousers and a shirt and shoes. Her husband picked his teeth with a match and hoisted his pants over his sagging paunch, not knowing that the clothes he had worn when he married her were on their way to Cape Town.

Bernard sighs. *I to get ready to go selling now. All the tourists go out driving today. I to see you later.*

We say goodbye. Raphael walks home because it's too late for a Rikki. The sun is coming up. It's Sunday. I go down to the flat and get into bed.

My body starts to shake. I try to stop my fear but I can't. I see a hundred white cut-out paper dolls which look like Mrs Rowinsky draped across the buildings. Red drips from the little round mouths of each one so they look like they are saying *O!* to something and burping blood. I can't rub out the image and then more and more seem to come at me, through my mind, filling up all the space in my head. They start to cry together in chorus: *O! O! O!*

I bury my head in my pillow to silence them. I leap up, run to the corner of the room, hunch over, try to get as small as possible. Black warriors and white Nazis come out of the cracks in the plaster, moving about, roving as bands, up and down corridors and deserted places. Their horses make no sound. A foul wind moves with them and their instruments of death, up and down, up and down, where the old packets and bits of paper blow.

The ground shakes, the earth trembles, drums pound. The light of the sun is hours away. It has not risen and even if it were high its light would not touch me now for the clouds are thick with the mist coming in. I hear Princess howling. The bodies of her daughters have been thrown onto a burning pyre. Their legs have been torn open and their baby breasts slashed with a panga.

Help me, Mossie! I crawl over and get into her bed. She puts her arms around me, holds me tight. I hear the armies marching. From a thousand miles away I hear them marching. From a thousand thousand miles I see pangas shining and tanks shining and automatic rifles shining. They catch the newly risen sun and flash it back into my eyes, blinding me for a moment.

Mossie pours beads over me. Words are tangled up in her throat. They won't untwine. They won't undo. They stay tied up but her panting tells me: *I hold you, I hold you.* She squeezes my face in her hands, forces my eyes open with her fingers so I look at her and understand from her noises and hugs: *I am here! I am here!*

Still the army marches. The earth rocks. Children are hidden everywhere. Some in the stones, some in the dry bushes which grow in these parts. Some are in the river pebbles. The stones will keep them safe for centuries. The stones will hold them until the earth has become still, until the quaking of the hills has ceased, until the marching armies march no more.

This picture, called *It is the Petrol for the Journey,* in which the brush moves tightly and forlornly, is of a plump, dark-haired, middle-aged woman standing at a Total petrol pump.

The woman holds the petrol pipe erect, like a cobra, about to fill a car's tank.

Beside her, on the right, is an image of her as a young girl with long, black hair cascading around her shoulders and a white dress billowing about her legs in the stirring wind.

Between and before them, so that he appears to be addressing both the woman and the young girl, kneels a handsome balladeer wearing a red scarf around his neck. His sleeves also billow in the wind.

In the right-hand corner we see a naked, black man with wings, flying towards the centre of the canvas, followed by a black bird with a yellow beak.

Chapter 33

Bernard walks with us to the Parade so Mossie can buy some beadwork. I bring her here every few months to buy from the traders who bring dagga in from the Transkei. The Nigerian told us about them. He doesn't waste his time with dagga, just deals hard drugs, but he knows all the networks and anyone who's moving anything.

Through him Mossie meets a whole crowd of rural people who don't speak much English but manage to communicate quite well. They buy up old beadwork in the Transkei for her and she is slowly building up a collection of Xhosa ceremonial beading. This is very old woven work, made into armbands, neckbands and other body ornaments.

We leave Mossie to do her own dealing for a good price and wait for her under King Edward's statue. We listen to a Bible reader raving on about the end of the world.

The dagga traders have explained the language of Xhosa beads to Mossie. Beads are not just coloured bits of glass. Beads, when woven together in different colour combinations, speak a language of their own. But this language is slowing dying because it is so old-fashioned and what beads once said, need no longer be spoken. Mossie is frantic to buy up this silent speech and earns lots of money watering Mrs Rowinsky's plants and brushing the Spice Girls' wigs.

She shows us her new pieces, lays some of them out on the steps under King Edward and dresses herself in others. She has a girdle beaded in green and orange; a neckband of pink, blue and white; a neck cascade and a matching set of leggings in bright turquoise, red, navy and white beads. These are very old pieces, threaded with sisal and caked with dried ochre. They say many things:

I am an old woman. I was once the best dancer but now my feet are tired. I am content to watch.

I am a Qaba maiden. I am not yet betrothed.

I have returned from working on the mines and my beloved awaits me; she has threaded this girdle for me for my homecoming.

I am a senior youth. At the dance of the young people I will select my maiden and invite her to be mine.

I have no child yet, but I am longing.

On the way home I tell Bernard to stop thinking about Morgana. It's dangerous business. It's one thing joking about getting minced into a salami by Giovanni if you look at his wife, but the truth is he'd kill you. Bernard is not after her for sex or anything. Bernard is happy just to look at her.

She be just the prisoner of that Mr Giovanni. You see him ever be kind to her? Always she just making the bread rolls and selling the pasta and I see her eyes they be too sad. I tired to see her in that shop.

Morgana is very white because she never goes out

of the shop or the upstairs flat. Her skin is like pale marble and she holds her pitch-black hair back with turtle-shell combs. Sometimes wisps come loose and fall about her face.

Morgana serves us one day and Bernard says something which makes her laugh. She laughs like a girl and puts her hand to her mouth, with eyes sparkling. He does not say you're beautiful, or shall we go out when what's-his-face is not looking. He just says something funny. Her laughter runs all through the shop. Her laughter, which was caused by another man, a black man, runs up Giovanni's spine and explodes in his head.

Giovanni screams out: *Whata you want, you black bastardo? Whata you want witha my wife? You pissa offa from my shop.*

He grabs his butcher knife, leans over the counter and pokes it under Bernard's chin.

You looka my wife I killa you! Black stronzo!

Bernard adjusts his hat, stands tall and sticks his chest out. I take him by the arm: Come, let's go. Mossie grabs his sleeve and pulls, stamping her feet. Bernard is not one for trouble but he's into dignity, so he doesn't rush out.

You first to sell me this the mozzarella rolls I order.

You want to die, Bernard? I say. Get real! We pull him out of the shop. Outside he starts to tremble. Not war-fever trembling. This is a new tremble.

You wanna fucka this black boy? You wanna this black merda to finga you? We hear Giovanni shouting at his wife in the shop. *You justa bitch! You filthy brutta puttana! You wanna black cock? I givva you black cock!*

We're standing outside the best shop in Long Street. Maybe we'll never go in again. The smells of black coffee and little Italian cakes waft out and over us. Why are we always getting thrown out of shops? I take Bernard's hand. Come, I tell him. Let's go home.

I to kill him, he hit his wife. He just like the rat, you see this? I to kill him.

Mmmh. Later, maybe. Let's go, I tell him again and me and Mossie steer him up to Skyline. Upstairs in his flat he leans over the balcony, smoking. We leave him alone and play poker on his sleeping mat. Mossie wins.

That night Giovanni snatches the cotton blouse and linen skirt from Morgana's body. He shakes her like a rag doll and her body is limp and crying. He throws her down on the bed and her cheek hits the headboard. He tears off his clothes and throws himself on her tender body, forcing himself into her privacy, cursing her because he knows she hates him. But she is his wife. She is his prisoner up there above the shop in Long Street.

There are three images of a woman in this untitled, unframed painting – a central one with two smaller ones in the background.

In the central image the woman sits at a window with a lace curtain stirring in the breeze. In the second she kneads bread dough. In the third we see her wiping a strand of hair from her face, leaving a trace of flour across her brow.

Soft, downward and seemingly penitent movements of dry termitary-browns and beiges (colours which give no sense of wetlands or moist places) interspersed with mango-yellow touches, convey a certain wistfulness and loneliness to the viewer.

Lined along the sides and edges and curving into the pattern of a snake are painted, in black and white, tins of tomato paste, basil pesto and olive oil.

Chapter 34

Weeks later me and Mossie and Bernard are sitting in the Whistle Stop Café. We've got the back table, sharing a plate of chips, dipping them into tomato sauce. Bernard is drinking beer.

On weekends Mossie paints her face with red ochre to go with her beaded headbands. She gets the ochre from her bead-sellers, who tell her traditional beads and red ochre must be worn together. I tell Mossie that if the New Horizons social worker ever sees her like this, she'll definitely be taken away, locked up, given pills. We won't save her with a lunch party a second time. Mossie's wearing a neck cascade and its strings of beads reach down to her toes. She stands up and shows me how she's supposed to toss the beaded streamers across her shoulder to hang over her bum, so they sway with her body movements. She wants me to know that's what she'll show the social worker if she ever comes snooping around.

Bernard laughs and orders more chips. *Little sister Mossie, you too sharp, really.*

She bangs the table and grins.

You know this Muslim Mr Achmat at the vegetables, number 20 Long Street? He the one who helping me when I come to Cape Town. He the one to give me the first job. I go with him all the days to the Epping Market and fetch the fruits and the vegetables. Then I to unpack in the shop and I help him to selling. I to shine up the tomatoes and apples and to make everything so fresh and nice. I soon to learn the English with him. You see my English too good. Yes? It can be I go to the English school. Yes?

We all laugh. Ja! Ja, sure. You could be a professor, Bernard. An English professor. Mossie drums on the table.

But I soon to be tired to polishing the apples, so I find myself these Chinese Warehouse and Mr Chan the Chinese merchant of the flags. And you see I make lots of money selling the flags. You see this the good business. Flags. What you thinking, little sister Mossie? You thinking this good thing?

Mossie hits the table and we all laugh. Bernard orders another beer and Cokes for us. He doesn't talk and for a while we are quiet at our table with our own thoughts in the smoky, broken light of the pub.

Bernard taught himself to write by copying the words from vegetable boxes. He prints his letters and sometimes gets them back to front.

You see my writing is the tomato writing. The first word I writing is TOMATO as I copy it from the box. Second word I writing is 2kg. Third word is KEEP CHILLED. Now I am writing anything as I like to. But the trouble is only that I to copy the words from somewhere. I cannot take the words in my mind to write them as I thinking them. If I want to write words as I thinking them I must tell someone to writing them down first. When I see the words with my eyes I can copy them the same way.

Mossie traces the word Coca-Cola on the can with her finger.

I to tell you something. I waiting for that day when the word I thinking in my mind, it just come out in the pen. So I not got to ask someone to show me that word first. Maybe you too lucky, you can do this already. Me, I can take grasses from the riverside and I can make a mat. You know this? I can make a nice mat with the weaving. I think maybe this the same thing to do with the words when you can write as you thinking.

The disco lights throb and we turn our chairs as the floor show begins. The music changes from disco to upbeat ballad. The lights dim and floodlights pick up Alice as she saunters onto the performers' platform in high, white, satin shoes and a white, satin gown buttoned at her breasts and falling about her long, slender legs. As she moves you see the shape of her thighs. She wears drop diamanté earrings and a wig of long, rich, black curls which tumble down her shoulders. Holding the microphone close to her mouth she sings an old Nina Simone number, swinging her body, moulding the air with her presence, holding the drinking audience spellbound with her sexual beauty.

Cliff and Gracie have a front table and they're both throbbing with the music. Gracie's glass eyes and Cliff's milk-white eyes look straight into the bright strobe lights without blinking. They're both drinking beer and by now they're a bit drunk. He's slapping his thigh and she's tapping her beer can. They look really trendy. Gracie is in leopard-print tights and a clingy strapless top, so all her creases and bulges show. Her big breasts heave. Cliff's wearing a scarlet, silk shirt and black trousers.

Alice and Bluebell got them dressing well. When they first moved into Skyline, Gracie wore straight-up-and-down skirts and blouses with sensible shoes and Cliff wore dull, badly-fitting suits. Blind school taught them how to dress in easy clothes with no eye for glamour.

Alice and Bluebell threw out their clothes and took Gracie and Cliff shopping for outrageous colours and textures. They brought in their dressmaker, Mrs Hendricks from Woodstock, to sew up some style. So now Gracie and Cliff have cupboards full of silks, satins, brocades, velvets and fake fur. In this way their Braille-sensitive fingers can read the cloth of their stunning clothes.

You don't have to see colour to be colour, Gracie dear. And frocks went out with the ark, so did these ghastly drip-dry synthetics. Crumple your velvets and let those satins sing! And as for that dreadful suit, Cliff, it looks like Brakpan 1969. Let's give it to the Salvation Army, hey?

They threw out the sensible flat shoes and bought platforms and boots. *Of course you won't fall, lovies, just walk tall and keep a hold on those harnesses. And if you take a tumble, so what? You'll look more gorgeous flat on your face in brocade than in tweed!*

Bluebell does Gracie's make-up every morning. She's taught Mossie how to paint Gracie's lips so they look succulent and her eyes so they invite you in. When Bluebell sleeps late at weekends, Mossie gets Gracie looking good.

Later, much later, after Alice's show, Bernard gets up slowly, feels whether his tie is straight, does up the middle button of his jacket and walks over to Giovanni, who is leaning up at the corner of the bar.

Bernard presses up behind him and pins him with his whole body to the counter. He pushes his head hard up against Giovanni's head so it's crushed against the wall. Giovanni's eye bulge a little and he tries to turn and pull out his knife. But Bernard's got him pinned in with his black body. He breathes hard on Giovanni's face. Black breath. The music is so loud Giovanni can only just hear what Bernard is saying. It's pounding and the strobe lights are breaking everything up into chips of movement. I see Bernard's movements chopped up by light. Giovanni is paralysed against the wall and the music blares on.

Suddenly Bernard lets off the pressure and Giovanni falls backwards, catches himself, looks around and walks out. Bernard watches him go, them comes back to us, dusts his lapel and sits down. He pours his beer slowly down his throat, then grins at us.

Come, we to go now.

What you tell him, Bernard?

I not want to tell you what I tell him. But he never make trouble again. I see that. He know this. When he hurt his wife next time I kill him.

In this painting, *It is the Saturday Night of Whistle Stop*, the artist uses reds and blotches of brown-yellows to convey a sense of noise, vibrancy and drunkenness.

Behind the bar and the barmaid, a large mirror reflects the crowded-together, smoking patrons captured with their drinks in mid-air or at their lips: vodka, cane spirit with Coke, rum and Castle beer.

In the mirror we see reflected the arching bodies of patrons moving to tinny township jazz and we almost hear the voice of a female singer cutting through towards, we imagine, heaven.

So energized is the movement here that we find ourselves swaying slightly, or at least lifting a hand in response to the rhythms and the Saturday-night smell of drink and sweat and cigarette smoke.

Two points differentiate this work from *The Bar at the Folies-Bergères*, by Edouard Manet, the painting on which it is based. The first is that this is a pub in Africa and not a nineteenth-century Parisian bar. The second is the barmaid's laughing countenance, so different from the pensive face of Manet's counterpart. Here we have a barmaid who is caught up by jazz and who has no sorrows upon which to reflect.

Chapter 35

I can smell the sea in the air. It smells of fish and salt and is cool and fresh.

I don't remember how the fight starts. Fights just start up, I suppose. It's in the quad at break time. I think she asks me what I'm looking at when she walks past. Maybe I ask her. Maybe she hits me first. I've forgotten. But I get her down and I'm smacking her against the ground. I'm hitting her but I'm really hitting our mother. Can you understand that? Everything just goes white in my mind and I'm hitting our mother over and over and over for wrecking my whole life. For making him leave us. For making our father leave us. I'm smashing up our mother against the tar in the quad but it isn't our mother. It's just a girl in my class who looked at me wrong.

They're pulling me off her. Raphael pulls me off and I hear him call my name again and again, shouting at me to stop: *Don't do this! Stop! Please!*

My head is white with pain and bursting. I want to cry but I won't. I look at my hands. I look at her face and the small trickle of blood coming out of her split lip. I look at the ground, at everybody's shoes standing around. And I walk away. I walk out of the school grounds and I walk home without ever looking backwards.

Raphael chases me and grabs me but I shake him

off. Leave me! Leave me! I never want to see you again! I hear teachers calling me back. I hear my name ringing in the air. But I just walk on.

I go up to the roof. I look across at the mountain and wish I could be on top. Just me and nobody else. Bernard is hanging up his washing. His linen shirts flap in the wind.

What you say? You say you home because you smash someone? You smash someone up in the school? Oh my! And your fellow? You leave Raphael? No! No! You don't cry. You listen me! You don't cry. You lie here on roof with me. You look up into sky. You see! Turn your mind a little bit, then you be looking down to sky, not up. Oh yes! It is so lovely. You see clouds but not up. This way you see clouds down. Just look the sky this way. You not to crying now.

Bernard spreads out cardboard and lies with me on the roof. We lie there while the sun gets hotter and hotter. We look at the sky facing down and watch the clouds and the pigeons and the seagulls below us. He holds my hand. The burning in my heart bursts and I cry so hard the clouds swim away and I see nothing, only blue and smudge. I cry so hard on the roof of Skyline that no more tears come and I turn to him to lie in his arms. He holds me close to him, with firmness and strength so the world might shatter but he will not let go. I feel his heart beat close to mine and smell the kind smell of his body mingled with his cologne. We go down to his flat and he lays out his sleeping mat for me. He strokes my face, closes my eyes, stills the brokenness in me so that I fall asleep.

When I wake up he is sitting on the floor near me, stirring sugar and sweetened condensed milk into hot tea and singing softly:

Vê como eu te busco,

Através do tempo inchado de passer,

Eu irei buscar-te no meu pequeno barco de tranças de

vinha.

Mas espera, só espera por mim.[3]

We drink the tea.

Now the fever gone from you. You see how the sky fix fever?

It is so sweet I feel sick. But it warms me up inside and I stop shaking. He gives me a jam doughnut sprinkled with sugar: *You to eat this now. You eat the sweetness to feeling better.*

Then we walk down to 7Eleven and lean against the window, waiting to fetch Mossie from the bus. Sylvester tells us to get our bodies off his glass, he's just cleaned it. We ignore him. I've got a headache.

---

[3] See how I will fetch you,

From across time swollen with passing,

I will fetch you in my small boat of plaited vines.

But wait, only wait for me.

In this painting we see a crimson angel tumbling from heaven. Her wide eyes show both terror and sorrow.

Soft, silken stains of terracotta and the grey-greens of lichen capture the fine weave of her garment.

Beneath the tumbling angel stand three figures with arms outstretched to catch her. In the centre is a black madonna dressed in a garment of faded, pink roses and green leaves.

On the right side is a young man and on the left stands a large, masculine-bodied woman, dressed in an emerald–green robe, reaching out to stop the angel's fall.

The painting is titled *The Angel is Crying* and follows Marc Chagall's *The Falling Angel* in texture and movement.

Chapter 36

I don't go to school. I don't care about the fight. I don't care what everyone thinks about me and I don't want to see Raphael. He doesn't come looking for me.

I meet Bernard after I take Mossie to the bus. He's on his way to the Buitengracht corner with his bags of flags.

I stay with you little time, yes? We eating the breakfast together. You be hungry?

We jump over the wall into the garden of the Lutheran church. Roses climb all over and oleander bushes hang heavy with soft, pink flowers. They remind Bernard of his wife's only dress. It was given to her by his Senhora to mark the visit of Cardinal João Paulo to the mission of the Sisters of Mercy not far from the ranch. Bernard's Senhora handed out old clothes to the workers. His wife took off her garment stitched from cloth meal-bags and put on a dress of roses.

The cardinal was driven from Lourenço Marques by a young, black priest to visit the Senhor and Senhora de Oliveira because they were generous patrons of the mission. He dropped the cardinal off at the ranch, then drove off through the hot dust to the Sisters of Mercy. The cardinal heard the confessions of the Senhor and Senhora in a small chapel built on the side of the house. He blessed them and gave them

Holy Communion. He prayed that their sons would come back safely from the war in Angola and that the drought would break.

Then the three of them sat down to feast on spit-roasted pork, duck, prawns from the warm Indian Ocean and delicious peri-peri chicken. The cardinal drank red wines and white wines and did not seem to notice the rich gravies dribbling from his mouth onto the white, linen serviette tucked under his chin. Bernard served silently, carrying each course through on silver platters and finally bringing to the table fresh mangoes and litchis soaked in liqueur and covered in thick cream.

The cardinal smoked cigars and drank coffee and burped into his double chin. He took a long rest in the cool guest-room, where he lay on a brass bed while flies buzzed against the window panes and cows mooed in the distance. Then he heaved his vast bulk out into the courtyard where the farm labourers had been waiting all day in the hot sun for him. He sat on a large, wooden chair, carved and inlaid with tiny ivory designs, and prayed over the workers.

Here in the Lutheran church garden I can make myself not hear the traffic. Sometimes I hear someone playing the organ inside the church. Huge tempests of sound come out from the stained glass windows and cover the traffic.

Why you fight now with your Raphael? He so fine fellow that young man. So good fellow.

I don't want to talk about him. It's finished now. I finish with him before he finishes with me. It's better like that. You don't get hurt this way.

I not understanding you so clear. You must hurt your nice fellow before he hurt you? That fellow no hurting nobody. Surely I say this.

Bernard unwraps bread and cheese he's bought from 7Eleven.

What you think I invite Mr Giovanni come drink tonight? We go Whistle Stop?

Don't try to make me laugh, Bernard. There's nothing funny about today. Can't you see I'm angry? I'm angry! Understand?

No! No! Surely I don't to make you laugh! And yes. I seeing it well you be angry. So come, we eat, we not to talking. I just be thinking. I not saying one more thing.

We eat in the shadow of the trees. I touch the roses. I want this to be my garden. We don't say anything. He sings:

Eu levanto-te como um copo vazio
Esquecido na margem do rio
E cheio do tempo sem fim do meu esperar por ti
Debaixo da lua e as estrelas e os sons de batuques.[4]

---

[4] I lift you like an empty glass
Forgotten at the river edge
And filled with the endless time of my waiting for you
Beneath the moon and stars and sounds of drums.

He stands up, dusts down his pants, straightens his jacket.

I to go now. I to see you later. Yes? But I to tell you just the one thing. No, I to tell you the two things.

Don't say anything, Bernard. I don't want to hear you preaching.

No. This not the preaching. You know me. I not the priest. This only to say I think you to go back to school. You so soon to finish. And then you be the writer of books as you wish. You see me with no school? And this other thing I to say is only I sorry for the troubles that happen. I so sorry.

He goes off to sell his flags. He stakes them all in the ground in a circle and they wave in the wind on the Buitengracht corner. Here are all the flags of the world, with him sitting in the centre like a president.

He's learnt from Mossie to feed birds. He makes neat little piles of seeds so the pigeons all have to peck in circles.

I stay here, on my back, and make my mind the way he taught me. I turn the sky around. I look down into the treetops, down into the roses, down into the blue where seagulls fly. I don't want to go back to school again. Ever.

This painting is of a garden and we are reminded of *Wall Painting from Villa of Livia, near Rome (late first century AD)*.

It is the only picture in the collection which does not make use of strong African colours and tones. The colours here are delicate, soft, translucent and dreamlike, and seem to caress the canvas.

The walled garden gives a sense that the viewer need merely step into it to be engulfed by the smell of roses and lavender, the taste of pomegranates, and the sweetness of orange. How easy too it is to hear the soft murmurings of pigeons.

Chapter 37

It's a hot, still night. Our mother has gone to bed. Mossie and I go down to eat with Cameron and the others.

Every night they make the same food: sadza, gravy and overcooked spinach. It's so nice you know why they eat it every day. Cameron shows us how to roll a little ball of sadza and dip it into the gravy. We don't use knives and forks here. They want to know why Raphael has stopped coming around. I say: Who's Raphael? We're talking history now.

Liberty is thumbing her mbira and the sound of her voice is a lament around the room. She does not form words, just throat and breast sounds. This is the sound of the plundered village. It is the after-sound of the village burnt to the ground, smouldering with the shot dead dogs lying around. It is the non-sound of a girl hiding in the bushes, turned to sand by fear.

Liberty's voice and the cry of the mbira are the sound of the girl's terror when the soldiers came. They are the sound of what she saw after days of hiding, when she came out of the bushes and saw the burnt bodies. They are the sound of her mother fused by fire to the body of her baby brother, embracing him, sheltering him from the crude flames of war.

The wire-workers are twisting wire and making fruit baskets and vegetable racks. Coils of wire are propped up against the wall in the lounge and all their stock is kept in big, red and blue plastic zip-up bags. Liberty's lament fills the room.

There's not much furniture here and nothing matches. It's not like anyone went out to Lewis Stores and bought a lounge suite. Everything came from here and there.

On the wall they've pasted pictures from magazines and this is one of the flats with newspaper stuck up on the windows instead of curtains. Also, their electricity got cut off, so they cook on a Primus stove and light candles. The flat smells of paraffin and glows softly.

Mossie shares out some sweets she got from Bluebell, then suddenly gets up and paces around the flat. Something's bothering her. She looks like a tracker dog out hunting.

What's up, Mossie? She drags me into the kitchen and stands dead still waiting for something, her hands held up in the air, ready to grab what she senses.

There's nothing here. Come. I pull at her. We hear a soft scritch-scratching. She lifts a curtain from under the sink and slides out a cardboard box. It has air holes and she knows immediately what's in there. She grunts frantically at me, opens the box and lifts out a live chicken. She holds it tightly to her chest, its legs tucked in, and closes her eyes. Then she spins round and marches angrily into the lounge. Liberty puts down her mbira. Beer bottles stop in mid-air. The candle flames flare up slightly.

Who boxed this chicken? Her whole body asks everyone. Who put this bird in a box under the sink without crumbs or water? Her angry face asks. Cameron and Liberty exchange glances. This chicken will be cooked tomorrow. That's the plan. Friday night supper. Chicken with sadza.

Cameron wants to tell her that it just flew in. That it just flapped by and landed on the veranda and clucked. There is nothing unusual about a chicken looking for a place to roost, but he can't lie to Mossie. So he just asks, calmly, as if he did nothing wrong, if it can live on the roof with her birds because the kitchen is not a good place to run around. She looks down at the bird and strokes its head, fiddles with its back feathers. She smiles at Cameron. You know how Mossie smiles. Everyone starts drinking again. We go back upstairs and for its first night with us the chicken sleeps with Mossie under her bed.

Once, there was a small, coloured child sleeping at Mossie's bus stop. He was all curled up on the bench holding tight onto a pack of sunflower seeds. She shook him awake and made me ask him who he was. His name was Raven. His big brother had dropped him off in town and told him to get on with life. When she heard his name, Mossie wanted to keep him. She kept pointing up at the roof, to show me he could live up there, in the storeroom where she kept her seeds.

Are you crazy? I shouted at her. How can you put

someone's kid in a hok on the roof? She grabbed him
and we had this tug-of-war with me trying to get him
loose and Mossie pulling him, and him trying to break
away. She clung to his arm, with her fingers going deep
into it, and he was crying. His little bag of seeds spilt
all over the place. Eventually I loosened him and he
ran away. She tried to go after him but I caught her and
took her back upstairs because there was no way she'd
calm down for school. We both stayed home. She was
very cross and sulked for a long time afterwards.

Now, tonight, she shows me that she has called the
chicken Raven, after that little kid. And she shows me
I should have let her keep him on the roof with her
birds because she would have looked after him well.

It's so hot I tie the curtains back. It's so hot and
the air is thick and poisoned with traffic fumes. Will
the wind from the top of the sea turn towards the
land? Will it stretch out and crawl up Long Street to
reach us up here? Will it drift up Long Street carrying
the smells of far away, of seaweed and merchant sea
vessels? Will it touch my face, cool me?

The intercom rings. It's Bernard. Why doesn't he
use his own key? Bernard, you lost your key? What's
up?

*I got my key. Oh yes. But someone here got no key. Some nice
fellow here to see you, got no key. I want to know I can send him
up? You can let him to come up?*

Bernard, are you talking about Raphael? I thought

I told you not to interfere in this. What do you mean, can you let him in? You let him in if you want. But then he visits you, right?

No, no. Listen me. This your good friend here. You know your good friend Raphael? He already coming up. I not to interfering, really. I just not like to see he has sorrow. I just go Whistle Stop have small beer now. So I say goodnight. Just I tell you, good friend cannot stop to be good friend. Just like I say. Good friend is good friend.

I wait on the landing. My legs tremble. What do you want, Raphael? Why are you here? You know I don't want to see you again. Can't you read the obvious? Must I explain it all in detail for you?

But I don't have to explain anything. He doesn't care what happened and who I want to beat up. He's just going to swim at Long Street Baths, that's all, because it's so hot that the tar is cracking, and if I want to come, that's great.

I want to go. But I don't want to go. But okay, it's hot. But don't talk about what happened. I don't want to talk about it, see? If you talk about what I don't want to hear, I'm just coming back.

I go in to Mossie and tell her I'm going out: You stay here, Mossie. Stay in the flat. Don't follow us.

She is lying under the bed with the chicken. There's chicken crap all over the carpet already. She rolls out from under the bed with a deep frown on her face and lies there looking up at me. She wants to know whether we should tell Mrs Naidoo that it was us who smashed her shop window. She's such a good friend now.

I'm not sure we should tell her, and anyway the insurance must have paid her. Let's leave things as they are for a while. We'll see what Bernard and Raphael think.

Mossie rolls back under the bed. She knows not to make noise and wake our mother up. I hear the chicken cluck softly. Raphael and I go round the back of the Long Street Baths and force open the small window we always climb through when we want to swim at night. The pool is still. There is no moon playing on the ocean water. We take our clothes off, take everything off, dive into the water which parts to let our bodies in.

We swim and dive and glitter. His body is wet and smooth and he kisses me, bends my body and kisses me and I visualize soft beach sand sprinkled with mother-of-pearl dust. I imagine coloured corals and water flowers, and fishes which know everything of the open ocean. Raphael. I swim from him. He catches me. We spiral down, down to the bottom where the pearls grow. We blow out all our air into bubbles and come up, up to the top, gasping and laughing.

From far away we hear the screeching of sirens but that is outside. Here we lie at the edge of our ocean where the kelp sways in a dance and the warm water currents mingle with the cold.

From here we do not see Mrs Rowinsky standing at her window in her long, white, lace nightgown, her silver hair loose and hanging down her shoulders, her sad eyes searching the night city, searching the roofs of Berlin, for the shadow of her father.

Here we do not know of those who toss and cry out in the night as flames enter their dreams and the sounds of gunfire pepper their sleeping. We know nothing of the clashes between rebels and government forces, of torched food stores, of landmines which wait in fields for unshod feet. We know not of the endless flowings of refugees who walk from one war to the next, from one country to the next, endlessly and through all time.

We know only the sparkling of our bodies and the laughing in our eyes and the wonderful touch of skin to skin.

This elegant work is styled on Gustav Klimt's *The Kiss*. The lovers are painted in the same exquisite patchwork of golds and luminous colours, although here the lovers are not as mature as Klimt's. We see a slight clumsiness in their embrace. However, one senses tenderness and youthful eroticism. There is a lovely beauty present.

Quite in contrast with the richness of the lovers'

garments, a simple spread of calabash-orange-brown covers the background.

There are no added images or floating objects and because of the lack of these devices the painting, when viewed in relation to the rest of the collection, seems to be incomplete.

Chapter 38

Bernard is lying on the roof looking up at the night sky. Mossie and me lie on each side of him and he holds our hands.

I to give you something tonight.

He smiles his soft smile.

You see the stars lying on the sky? These the same stars I see in Mozambique. These my wife's stars. These stars for you and little sister Mossie and for your fine fellow, Raphael. All the stars of my wife, I share them to you. Little sister Mossie, look up! You see stars are beads of the sky. These the star beads from Mozambique. From before the war.

My wife throw her beads up into the sky when the war comes to Mozambique. My wife take those beads from her neck and she throw her beads up into the sky so they to become stars. She tell my childrens, maybe we not see each other again. Maybe the war take us all away. So she throw her beads into the sky for when we far away we can look at those beads and still remember each other. They to remember my childrens. My Augustinho. My Mateus. My Roberto.

Tears come out of the corners of his eyes and run down his face. Little silver rivers. He says his children's names again: *Augustinho. Mateus. Roberto.*

Mossie lies with her head on Bernard's shoulder, his arm around her, her chicken tucked tightly under her arm. It is a very calm chicken. It knows how close it came to a cooking pot death and is content to be dragged around without fussing.

Mossie looks up at the great bead shop of the sky. She lifts her arms and the chicken flaps. Then she tries gently to touch the star beads from Mozambique and starts counting them, one by one. Soon she will know the pattern of the whole sky by heart.

Bernard points to the stars and tells her she must leave them there.

These the beads of forever. No good to put them in the bottles. They not be shining in the bottles. You keep the small glass beads in the bottles. These the star beads you leave in the sky. Just you look at them. And you be pleased always because they so beautiful.

Bernard moves Mossie gently to one side. I sit up and he kneels in front of me. The chicken flaps up then settles again.

He takes my face in his hands. His eyes search my face, move from my mouth across my cheeks to my eyes.

I to tell you something. I to tell you the first time I see your face, before I even to know your name, I see in your face these stars of my wife and childrens, they shining in your eyes. I see the moon and those stars are some things you bring back to my dark life. I never to lose them again. Only I show them to you now. I give them to you, so your life never to be dark. And you to look after them for my wife and childrens. So they not losing the road to find each other.

He takes my hands in his and I watch the rivers run down from his eyes and I watch the stars reflecting in them and the fish jumping and the little brown terrapins swimming by.

He pulls a chocolate slab out of his pocket and breaks it up into squares and we sit there on the roof the whole night eating chocolate, waiting for Mossie to count the stars.

This painting is of a black, peasant woman crawling on her hands and knees towards a group of soldiers. Her faded dress is brushed with suggestions of roses and leaves. In addition to this often-used image of a faded, floral dress we see another of the recurring images, that of a black bird with a yellow beak flying across the top of the canvas.

It is the end of a military manoeuvre and the soldiers, dressed in camouflage fatigues, stand around smoking and laughing. It is clear to the viewer that they will shoot the woman later.

In the background, a mission smoulders in reds and golds.

In the foreground are a child's lost shoe and a broken crucifix.

To the right sits a cardinal wearing a scarlet robe and black sunglasses. He is holding a bottle of Madeira wine and a goblet.

A roasted piglet floats by.

Chapter 39

Bernard has two beers at the Whistle Stop Café. He doesn't stay long but, because the night is hot, he strolls down Long Street looking in at all the clubs and pubs, drifting along on the vibes and noise. He's going to meet us later on the roof.

The traffic drowns the footsteps behind him. The street lights shimmer into the shadows so the three men who corner him easily bundle him down the dark lane alongside Kennedy's Cigar Bar. They pin him to the wall. He hears the crackling of boots against the dry scrub and bushes. He hears the smothered cries of mothers running. He hears the shouts of soldiers behind him. Three armies circle him and he begins to sweat the cold waters which the closeness of death brings. He smells the acrid sweat of killers; feels the silver texture of guns against flesh, pangas against flesh, war against the beauty of non-war.

We are up on the roof and we know nothing, me and Raphael and Mossie. We are on the roof waiting for Bernard to meet us here. We do not know that his mind has opened up like a calabash, spilling its seeds of controlled nightmare, and that the three marching armies have circled him outside Kennedy's; that the horror of his war has found him at last. War will seek you out. War will wear any garment to come find you if you flee from its killing fields.

Adelaide and Chris are lying on their spread-out cardboard boxes at the end of the lane. They see the swift killing-act through their meths-soaked eyes: a few brisk movements, the deep thrust of a cruelly sharpened knife, a soft gasp.

Bernard's beautiful eyes search for help in the shadows. They scour the undergrowth, afraid that we too might be trapped here in this valley of death; afraid that we too have been herded off with the countless others into the camps and enclosures for child-soldiers. He hears Giovanni hiss hotly into his face: *Black bastardo! You want looka my wife again? I showa you my wife, you black merda!*

Adelaide and Chris watch the shapes of the three men swagger their way out of the lane and back into the people-flow of Long Street. They see the shape of the Sultan stride off and leap into a four-by-four parked up on the pavement. They see the shadow of Sylvester cross Long Street and lean up outside Bliss Café. They watch the blur of Giovanni move towards a hooker standing against the corner lamp. She is stroking her thigh, stroking the inside of her leg, pouting her lips, sucking at her finger. They see Giovanni press against her and lick her cheek, squeeze one of her breasts and slide his hand up her leg.

But they don't see this straight up and down. They see this all broken and far away, as if they are under water, in a pool, and outside of it something vague and glimmering is going on.

Through their lane and across their sleeping space a river runs: red ochre which cannot soak into the earth because of the tar; scarlet which is crying; crimson which prints onto the tar a lake of velvet, clotted blood.

Chapter 40

Bernard painted his last picture a week before he was killed, from the second-floor veranda of the Pan African Market. From there you can see Skyline quite clearly. He propped up his easel and worked for a full day, without a shirt on, drinking beer, sweating in the sun, shaded by the broad brim of his hat, while Raphael and me took Mossie to the swollen shack-lands of Khayelitsha to trade her old clothes for beadwork.

After Bernard was killed Mrs Rowinsky catalogued all his work and set up an exhibition at the National Gallery. She thought it was better not to sell any of his paintings but to keep the collection complete. Some are on permanent exhibition at the Gallery and the Pan African Market. The rest are shared among her, me and Mossie, Alice and Bluebell, Cliff and Gracie, Cameron and Liberty, Princess and the sweet-sellers.

When he died in that alley, all alone, we were waiting for him on the roof, waiting while the moon rose and set and the sun rose in its place. Princess found him, as she had once found Alice, and brought him home. Princess from Rwanda picked him up in her great, black arms and placed him on Alice's white couch. She knew better than anyone how to carry the war-dead, how to wade waist-deep through rivers tight-jammed with bloated bodies floating down to the sea.

I knelt beside the white couch as the river she had

carried him through burst its banks, flooded, tore me away and carried me down, down to the wastelands and threw me up onto rocks. Crocodiles rose from the river edge and circled me. I was left alone, the last one alive, trapped in killing fields among silent, broken dolls. I stumbled over the million war-dead children, their eyes of glass asleep now.

I called out to Bernard with my voice of screeching birds, demanding a return, crying for his homecoming, while Princess of Rwanda held my head to her great, soft breasts and rocked me.

Aih! Aih! Aih! My daughters and the one you love, they cannot return. We cannot call them back from where they are. They can only look upon us. My daughters and the one you love, they have gone! You understand what I tell you?

She wiped my face with the palms of her hands and held a mug of her brewed tea to my dry lips.

You be still now. You stop calling him. You stay here where we are the living. This not your time now to follow. We keep you here with us. The dead, they are gone. There is no raft for us to fetch back my daughters and the one you love. You only can wish for them some peace. Aih! Aih! Aih! Drink now what I give you. Drink it.

Princess held me in her big arms while time came and went. She forced a quietness to settle. She held me until the black crows of grief left me and sat on naked branches without sound; until the river became a dry bed once more; until in the distance I saw Mossie and Raphael coming to lift me up and carry me back home.

Sometimes I glimpse Bernard, fleetingly, in the Lutheran church garden, when the wind is silent and the shadows of leaves show no movement; when there is a sparkling of sun upon the dark and light greens of foliage.

And sometimes, when the caress of Long Street traffic becomes that of the mothers of the dispossessed, affirming the dreams and hopes of those who have walked down Africa, I might hear Bernard's song at the intersection:

Assim é como eu te amarei de longe:
Eu darei um beijo ao vento
Eu apanharei nas minhas palmas todas as estrelas que
*   caem,*
Para que nenhuma se perca.
Abraçarei os meus pensamentos de ti,
Para que o meu amor possa encher a terra
E durar até ao fim dos tempos.[5]

And I might turn towards where his song is coming from, amidst all the roaring, and call out from the traffic island in the middle of Long Street: Bernard!

---

[5] This is how I will love you from afar,
I will kiss the wind
I will catch in my palms all stars which fall,
So none are lost,
I will embrace my thoughts of you,
So that my love will fill the earth
And last till the end of time.

Bernard! Look at me! I am a writer now. I can spin my words, my many gathered words, into fine coir and threads of raw cotton, as you always said I should, so as to weave from them all manner of finery.

Bernard! I can weave from my words histories and songs of love, rhyming sculptures and pictures of every sort! They fly in the wind for you! Do you see them? Not concrete, not traffic fumes! They are no longer vagrant and wandering words. They are tales, Bernard, tellings which the wind will always carry for you!

Or I might sit on the roof with Raphael, on spread out cardboard, drinking Coke, waiting while Mossie feeds her birds, and I might whisper into the wind: Yes, Bernard! We are the guardians of your wife's stars. We watch them and count them in the darkness of night. They will never go out, for we will keep them alight forever.

This, the largest of the paintings, is done in oils of bright, vibrant colour and has an extravagance of emotion which never escapes the artist's control.

It depicts a girl sitting on the floor of the veranda of a rundown block of flats. Her legs dangle through the rails. From the rails hangs a South African flag and through this the artist has captured the slight movement of an easterly wind.

She is wearing an overlarge, man's jacket and holds her hair back with a tie.

Her face, painted with supreme delicacy and restraint, reminds one of the open savannah of central Africa. It has the colour of the fine, white dust churned up by disturbed herds of galloping antelope. It is a strong face with a half-smiling, slightly disgruntled mouth.

Beside her stands a younger girl, her head thrown back laughing as a flock of pigeons hovers to her right.

She too holds her hair back with a man's tie. Around her neck hang strands of carnelian, ebony and Ethiopian silver beads. A gold-brown hen sits at her feet, with an egg at its side.

To the left stands a young man wearing a broad-brimmed panama hat and sunglasses. He has his hands in the pockets of a beige, tailored jacket, one leg slightly forward, a crocodile-skin belt holding up the elegant trousers of his suit. The buttons of his white shirt are open, suggesting a slight eccentricity.

Propped up on an easel is an artist's palette smudged with vibrant oils of aloe-crimson, shadowed-chameleon-green and butterfly-mauve.

In the left corner is a copy of *The Essential Guide to Western Art.*

In the background we see a framed painting of a broadly smiling black man wearing a red beret.

The title, *It is the Portrait of the Artist with his Good Friends,* is printed on the right.

The frame of this, the last painting in the Bernard Sebastião Collection, is made of small stars cut from old tin.

The End

Glossary

Bakkie (Afrikaans) Container or basin

Barbel Large, slimy, fresh-water mud fish with fleshy filaments hanging from its mouth, of the genus Barbus

Bergie (Afrikaans) A vagrant. Originally name given to homeless people living on slopes of Table Mountain, but now commonly used for people living rough in the city

Caprivi Strip A narrow strip of Namibia that abuts Angola Botswana and Zambia which was the theatre for a number of crucial battles for control of the region

Checkers (South African English) A double-handled plastic supermarket bag. From itsheka, Xhosa adaptation of Checkers, the name of a supermarket chain

Chimurenga war (Shona) Zimbabwean war of liberation

Coloured A term used under apartheid to denote people of mixed race. Pejorative when used to discriminate, but generally not considered offensive when used in a cultural context

Doek Head scarf or cloth tied about the head

Dop A tot; a little drink, usually of spirits

DP Democratic Party. Opposition to the ruling ANC government of South Africa

Frelimo Mozambique Liberation Front. Guerrilla movement which overthrew Portuguese colonial rule in Mozambique

General Magnus Malan Head of South African security forces during 1970s and 1980s

Hotnot An offensive mode of address or reference to a coloured person

Ian Smith's Army Rhodesian troops entered neighbouring socialist Mozambique to destabilize it and to hunt out forces it perceived to be hostile. Ian Smith, as Prime Minister of Rhodesia, declared independence from Britain through UDI (Unilateral Declaration of Independence)

Illegals Illegal immigrants. Particularly those who arrive from the rest of Africa

Kapenta Dried, tiny, fresh water fish. A staple food

Koppie (Afrikaans) (Also kopje Dutch spelling). A flat-topped or pointed hillock

Kwere kwere (Xhosa or Zulu) Foreigner living in South Africa illegally. Often a derogatory term and generally referring to black Africans

Kwaito African urban fusion music

Lourenço Marques Former name, until the end of Portuguese colonial rule in 1976, of Maputo, Mozambique

MPLA Movement for the Popular Liberation of Angola. Won the first free elections and was soon immersed in a civil war with Unita rebel forces

Mbira (Shona) Musical instrument played with the thumbs, either over or inside a calabash

Meths Methylated spirits. Alcohol impregnated with methanol to make it unfit for drinking and exempt from duty. Even so, often drunk by destitute alcoholics as a cheap substitute for alcohol

Moffie Homosexual, sometimes a male transvestite. Derogatory term

Mtoki Food staple prepared from bananas

Panga A large broad-bladed knife used for heavy cutting of bush, and as a weapon

Qaba The amaQaba have not adopted Western religion and ways and still adhere to pre-Christian dress, beliefs and practises. The name literally means heathen. They paint themselves and their attire with red ochre

Renamo Mozambique National Resistance Rebel Movement supported by South African apartheid government to destabilize Mozambique

SABC South African Broadcasting Corporation

Sadza Thick porridge made from maize, millet or sorghum

Slim people Persons suffering from AIDS particularly in the last, terminal stages of the disease

Stompie Cigarette butt

Unita Angolan rebel movement set up against the MPLA government and backed by United States and apartheid South African forces and led by Jonas Savimbi until his death

Vetkoek (Afrikaans) A cake usually of yeast dough, deep-fried and similar to a doughnut though usually not sweetened

Vrot (Afrikaans) Rotten

Yvonne Chaka Chaka Popular, award winning and internationally renowned South African singer, born Yvonne Machaka in 1965

Xhosa AmaXhosa. African people originally from present day Eastern Cape

Bibliography

Branford, Jean and Branford, William. *A Dictionary of South African English*. Oxford University Press, Cape Town, 1991

Beckett, Sister Wendy. *The Story of Painting – The essential guide to the history of western art*. Dorling Kindersley, London, 1994

Lake, Carlton and Maillard, Robert (General editors). *A Dictionary of Modern Painting*. Methuen and Co. Ltd. London, 1956

Marsh, Jan. *Pre-Raphaelite Women*. Weidenfeld and Nicolson, London, 1987

Polonsky, Gill. *Chagall*. Phaidon Colour Library, London, 1998